"HERE'S TO THE STRIPPERS!"

Earl yelled out, "How about a last strip in the governor's mansion, Blaze?"

I jumped up on the table. All the other girls were standing around the table, clapping their hands and yelling, "Take it off! Take it off!" On the radio, Elvis Presley was singing, "You ain't nothing but a hound dog."

I threw my clothes in every direction until I stood there, stripped to my panties, dancing the last dance in the mansion for Earl. Two or three of the other girls started dancing and stripping, and within the next ten minutes, they had all stripped down to their panties. Earl loved every minute of it. He held his Coke bottle up and said, "Here's to the strippers! Here's to the state of Louisiana! Here's to Earl Long! May he live forever!"

BLAZE STARR

My Life as Told to Huey Perry

Blaze Starr
and
Huey Perry

Afterword by Lora Fleming

POCKET BOOKS

New York   London   Toronto   Sydney   Tokyo

POCKET BOOKS, a division of Simon & Schuster Inc.
1230 Avenue of the Americas, New York, NY 10020

Copyright © 1974 by Praeger Publishers, Inc.

Published by arrangement with Henry Holt and Company, Inc.
Library of Congress Catalog Card Number: 73-9392

ISBN 0-671-69665-3

First Pocket Books printing December 1989

10 9 8 7 6 5 4 3 2 1

POCKET and colophon are registered trademarks
of Simon & Schuster Inc.

Printed in the U.S.A.

To our mothers and fathers

FOREWORD
By Huey Perry

Anybody born and raised in the hills and hollows of West Virginia knows that to survive, there or anywhere else you travel away from home, you've got to be ready all the time to use all your resources. Anybody from Appalachia also feels a real tug towards home all the time. Some, like Blaze Starr, go away to work and settle down elsewhere but take every opportunity that comes along to go back to visit with their relatives and friends. Some go away to work or to school but come back to settle, as I did after I got out of Berea College and Marshall University and went home to teach history in high school and later run the antipoverty project in Mingo County during Lyndon Johnson's ill-fated War on Poverty.

It was while I was working for the Office of Economic Opportunity in Mingo that I happened to learn that the famous stripper Blaze Starr was born Fannie Belle Fleming in a lonely hollow up Twelve Pole Creek near Wilsondale. Later, I met Blaze for the first time at the Two O'Clock Club in Baltimore and got the idea that I'd like

7

to write her story. After hours of taped interviews and weeks of writing, I have finally completed the life of Blaze Starr as told to me by her.

The true events of Blaze's life are enough to defy the imagination of the most vivid fiction writer. Born during the Depression of the 1930s in the head of Newground Hollow in the backwoods of West Virginia, she was determined not to remain a beleaguered, poverty-stricken mountain woman. And through sheer determination and in conflict with her fundamentalist upbringing, she escaped the hardships of Appalachia by making use of her most formidable resource, her body.

As she moved through the heartland of America in defiance of the moral codes of its major cities, she left police departments stunned and the Daughters of the American Revolution shocked as their sons of Harvard cut classes to hear Blaze call them "you little evil ol' tomcats."

A hellfire-and-damnation preacher from Twelve Pole Creek claimed, "She has wedded her soul to the devil. No decent woman would ever think about making a living by parading naked in front of a bunch of men!"

Invading Bourbon Street in New Orleans at the peak of her career, she and Governor Earl K. Long picked up the state of Louisiana and shook it by its heels.

Today she lives on Baltimore's Queen Anne Road and reigns supreme over the city's notorious Block at the Two O'Clock Club, where she stripped for the second time and which she now owns. The Block is a seedy, run-down, block-long street in East Baltimore. Russell Baker in a recent *New York Times* Sunday magazine article called it "Blaze Starr's ruined kingdom." By her friends she is known as the Mayor of the Block. "Blaze Starr could be elected mayor of Baltimore," I was told by the cabbie who drove me to the edge of her black iron picket fence in the suburbs.

To my delight I found Blaze Starr to be an intelligent,

charming, delightful woman, with a warm sense of humor about life and herself. Her native state of West Virginia can take pride in this celebrated daughter. I have enjoyed immensely the past year of working with her and writing her story. It tickles me to say that without her this book would not have been possible. Two other charming and powerful women also helped to make this book possible, however, and I want to acknowledge them too: They are my devoted wife, Shirley, on whom I relied for suggestions and ideas, to say nothing of all the typing and retyping of the manuscript, and Lois Decker O'Neill of Praeger Publishers' Washington office, the most skillful and enthusiastic editor a writer could hope to have. All three, as we say down home, are real mean women.

Charleston, West Virginia
February 1974

BLAZE STARR

1

Other than coon hunters and revenuers, very few people have ever set foot in Newground Hollow. Just what led my mother and father to make their way from Twelve Pole Creek following the night of their marriage to the head of this little hollow where they built a two-room log cabin and raised all eleven of us young'uns, I guess remains something of a puzzlement to most people who knew about it.

Anyway, I am sure my father, Goodlow Fleming, and my mother, Lora, knew exactly what they were doing, for there in that little West Virginia hollow I lived the first fourteen years of my life as happy and contented as any child could be. Sure, there were hardships. The winters were rough. Sometimes the snow would lay on the ground from November through March, and it was always a task getting up in the middle of the night and running a hundred yards down the hill to the outhouse in near zero weather. But jumping back into that warm featherbed with my sisters and pulling the cover over my head was a pleasant experience I shall never forget.

Our closest neighbors were two miles away, and the only way in and out of the hollow was a foot path that paralleled the stream, crisscrossing it occasionally by means of logs or a narrow swinging bridge as it meandered down the mountain hollow until it intersected Twelve Pole Creek. Tall poplars and huge red oaks lined the stream banks, and deer would come down out of the forest to water just below what we called Slick Rock Falls. Squirrels were constantly barking as they chased each other through the trees. Of course, you had to be alert for the singing of a mountain rattler and you had to keep your eyes peeled for copperheads. My daddy taught me always to carry a hickory stick to part the weeds, especially when my sister, June, and I went every evening to fetch our two cows, who sometimes strayed a mile or two from the cabin. I whacked many a copperhead with that hickory stick.

I guess hunting the cows is where I developed such a keen sense of hearing. Daddy had tied bells around old Sally and Betsy, and as they chomped the grass, the bells clanged so that we could locate them from the direction of the sound. Occasionally, they got stubborn and stood silently, but we soon learned to track them and never failed to find them. I honestly believe it was a game old Sally and Betsy would play with June and me, for just as soon as we got within sight of them, they would break and run towards the house. When we had difficulty finding them, we always feared that maybe one or even both of them had disappeared down a sinkhole—those scary, mushy drainage places in the woods that led down to worked-out coal mines or underground streams. I never really heard of any animal or person disappearing down a sinkhole, but one of our relatives had a cow that broke a leg falling in one and had to be shot, and there were stories a-plenty to send shivers down a child's back. The most chilling one concerned a "woman-ick," a black panther-like beast that lived in a sinkhole and roamed the hills of Twelve Pole Creek devouring everything it came across, including little children. All the folks called it a "woman-ick" because of its shrill, bloodcurdling scream that would echo down the valley. I only heard it once or twice, but that was enough to keep June and me scared half out of our wits when we were cow-hunting. We wouldn't even think about getting within a hundred yards of a sinkhole.

Grandma and Grandpa Fleming lived over in another hollow almost ten miles from Newground Hollow. It was always a big thrill to visit with them, especially if Grandpa John was getting ready to make a run of moonshine. To get to their place, we had to walk along a mountain trail that eventually passed through a low gap that led from Newground Hollow to Chestnut Hollow, then down Chestnut Hollow for about three miles where we turned left up another hollow and followed a mountain path that wound its way into the head of the Old Fork of Jenny's Creek.

All the people in the valley called my grandpa "Ol' Twelve-Toed John Fleming." He was of German descent, and sure enough he had six toes on each foot. He never wore shoes except in the wintertime, and then it was a huge pair of gummed overshoes that would accommodate his six toes comfortably. He was stockily built for a man in his sixties and certainly looked much younger. He wore blue overall pants and a blue cotton shirt. His eyes squinted as if he was looking far in the distance, and his normal three weeks' growth of stubble complemented his high cheekbones. He and my grandmother, Elizabeth, had raised twelve children in their small three-room cabin.

One particular visit to Grandpa Fleming's shall always remain vivid in my memory. It was late in the fall of 1940. My older sister, June, my younger brother, Ray, and I made the trip through the woods. It was one of a sort we had made many times in the past. Grandpa had sent word by my Uncle Garfield about a week earlier that he would be needing us, and we all knew what that meant.

As we arrived at the cabin that day, Grandpa John was sitting in his rocker on the front porch. Two of his three fox hounds were lying nearby, and Grandma Elizabeth was busily churning milk. The dogs began to bark when we approached as they were trained to do when anyone neared the house.

I yelled out, "It's us, Grandpa, me, June, and Ray."

He raised up out of his rocker and said, "I declare! I wasn't expecting you kids until late tomorrow. I just got back from checking the mash, and it looks like it's going to have to work another day or two before we can make the run. Well, anyway, that's all right; I've got a lot of other things we can take care of while we are waiting."

Grandma stopped churning and hurried to the front gate to greet us. She was a kind and gentle woman, a picture of beauty with her long silver hair plaited into a bun and fastened at the back of her head. "You children must be starved," she said as she ran her fingers through Ray's hair.

"Well, I guess we could stand a mighten to eat," June replied. "Sure hope you have some gingerbread."

"We'll see about that. In the meantime, why don't you draw some fresh water from the well and get yourself a drink and wash your face and hands." She secured her apron and walked into the kitchen.

Old Blue was sniffing and growling at Ray, and Grandpa yelled out, "Get on off, Blue, and leave the boy alone. He's plumb give out 'cause that's a long walk for a five-year-old." I don't know whether Old Blue understood Grandpa, but he went back to the porch and lay down as if his feelings had been hurt.

A few minutes later, we were all sitting at Grandma's table eating gingerbread and drinking sassafras tea. A pot of squirrels was stewing on the stove, and Grandpa grinned from ear to ear as he reminded us that we were going to have squirrel for breakfast. I never cared too much for squirrel, but I could eat my weight in squirrel gravy, especially with Grandma's homemade biscuits.

Their cabin was as isolated as ours. The nearest neighbor was almost three miles away. All my uncles and aunts had grown up, married, and moved on to another hollow with the exception of Aunt Dora and Uncle Garfield who were still at home. Uncle Garfield was about twenty years old at the time and was always gone—either off somewhere hunting or courting one of the Marcum girls over on Twelve Pole Creek.

Three days passed before the mash was ready to run. Grandpa got up early that morning, milked his cow, and had the fire built in the cookstove before the first rooster crowed. Shortly thereafter, I could hear the pots and pans begin to rattle, and I knew Grandma was fixing breakfast. I roused June, and we began to dress.

Grandpa came into the kitchen carrying an armload of chestnut firewood and dumped it into the woodbox behind the stove just as I stuck my head through the curtains of the doorway. ''Well, Sissie, it sure looks like a good day to start the run. There's a low fog, and them revenue men are going to have a hard time separating the smoke from the fog,'' he chuckled. Everyone in the family had always called me ''Sissie.'' Only rarely did anybody use my real name, Fannie Belle.

Grandpa was a notorious moonshiner, and to prove it, he had already spent five years in prison when my daddy was a young boy. To him making corn liquor was an art, and the neighbors for miles around knew when they were drinking moonshine made by Ol' Twelve-Toed John Fleming. His mash was always made from corn, and he never tried to hurry it up like some of the moonshiners in the area who mixed hog middlin's with the corn, then added soap lye to get the fixin's to ferment faster. No sir, he took his time and just sat back and let nature take its course. His equipment was important to him, too. He always used a copper kettle and a copper worm so there wouldn't be any danger of poison, which was common when moonshine was made in zinc kettles.

You had to be careful in buying the granulated sugar that was mixed with the corn to make the mash. The revenuers were always snooping around the grocery stores trying to find out who had just purchased a large quantity of sugar. But Grandpa outsmarted them. He would take the time to buy his sugar from eight or ten stores. Sometimes he would be gone a week just buying sugar. Grandma always complained that it cost him more to get the sugar than he made off the moonshine.

Aunt Dora came in and joined us at the breakfast table. Uncle Garfield had taken the two hounds on a hunt the night before and hadn't shown up yet. Grandma said he sometimes stayed gone for three days.

"All right, you kids bow your heads. Grandma will turn thanks." We all bowed our heads.

"Dear God, we thank you for our lives. Bless all our children and grandchildren. Bless this food, and may we all have a good day. Amen."

As soon as breakfast was over, Grandpa and I headed for the still. My job was to find a good vantage point about a quarter mile from the still and watch for the revenuers. The site I always selected was a huge oak tree that stood almost alone atop a rock cliff that overlooked the valley. In the summer you could see for a mile in almost any direction, and in the winter months when the leaves were off the trees, the view was just about endless.

Sitting there in that big oak tree I really felt a part of nature. For hours I could watch a squirrel play in the tree limbs or a chipmunk digging in the leaves for nuts. When I tired, I would climb down out of the tree and look for ginseng.

Spotting ginseng is another art, just about as special as making good moonshine. The leaves change color with the changing light, and it is very difficult to find. One of the most disappointing moments comes when you step over a big four-prong ginseng about the same time someone behind you spots it. Most of the people in the valley would only ginseng during the fall of the year when the berries turned a bright red and the plant was easy to locate. The roots were dried out and later sold by the pound at the grocery store for medicinal use by the local people or to traveling buyers who came to the hills to stock up on it and furs and other mountain items.

Sometimes I sat in the tree near the still and played my harmonica, but any strange sound or rustling of leaves would always catch my attention. On this particular day, however, I slipped. Late in the afternoon, I suddenly discovered that I had allowed three strangers to get in quite close unnoticed, and when I did catch sight of them, they were less than a hundred yards from me. I was terrified as I yelled, "Run, Grandpa, they are right on top of us!"

My first inclination as I climbed down out of the tree was to go talk to the men and see if I could divert their attention from the still. But as soon as I attempted to strike up a conversation with the three of them, one picked me up, put me on his shoulder, and moved on towards the still. I realized then that they knew exactly where it was. Someone had squealed on Grandpa for certain.

When we reached the still, Grandpa was nowhere in sight. He had run up the hill and hid in the blackberry patch. I knew that no one was going to find him there. Nevertheless, I was scared to death.

The man who had carried me up the hill yelled out, "Hey, Twelve-Toed, come on out of there or we are going to take your little girl."

I began to cry and tried to pull away, but the man held firmly to my wrist.

After waiting a few minutes, one of the revenuers suggested that it might be proper to sample the find, so he took the dipper Grandpa used to cut the corn liquor, poured out a healthy drink, and proceeded to pass it around. It must have been 150 proof because Grandpa had not had a chance to cut it down by adding the proper amount of water.

"Goddamn, that's hot liquor," he said as he jumped for the water bucket, turning it up and drinking two large gulps to cool his throat.

"Yeah, it's hot," replied his buddy, "but it's damn good liquor," and he too reached for the bucket.

The man who was holding on to my arm glanced down and said, "Girl, I am going to turn you loose, but you'd better not try to run. You hear me?"

I nodded and sat down on a rock next to the still. A gallon jug stood under the copper worm, and the whiskey dripped slowly.

Occasionally, one of the men would yell out, "Hey, Ol' Twelve-Toed, we got your little girl, and we know you are here. So come on out, and let's get it over with."

There was no reply from Grandpa, and I knew they were not going to find him. He had told us many tales about the years he had spent in prison, and he always vowed that they would never take him there again.

The three men continued to sample Grandpa's whiskey. One of them was even kind enough to throw wood on the fire when it burned low. They seemed to be having a good time, joking and laughing and passing the dipper around. All was going well, and I thought perhaps they would just go away and leave us alone until I heard Old Blue come running and barking up the path towards the still. I knew he would lead them to Grandpa, so I grabbed him before he could break away and pretended to be playing, hoping they would not notice my anxiety.

"God, that's a good-looking dog," one of the men said. "Bet he would like a drink of Ol' Twelve-Toed's liquor."

"Why, hell yeah, he would. Why do you think he's come running up here? He has smelled this liquor and wants a drink." The man staggered to his feet, poured the dipper half full of moonshine, and said, "Here, dog, have a drink. It's the best goddamn moonshine in West Virginia. Come on, take a drink, and we'll all howl at the moon."

He held the dipper down to Old Blue's nose, and the dog began lapping the liquor. I could hardly believe it; I had never heard of a moonshine-drinking dog. Fifteen minutes later, Old Blue's eyes rolled back in his head; and he fell over, groaned a little, and began to snore. I was relieved, for I knew Old Blue could never lead them to Grandpa now.

The drinking continued for another hour or so, and finally the three men joined Old Blue. They had all passed out and lay spraddled on the ground. A few minutes later, I saw Grandpa sneaking down the hill on all fours. I jumped up and ran to him to explain what had happened.

All Grandpa could say was, "Well, I'll be doggoned. I'll be doggoned." He came on down to the still, took his foot, and rolled one of the men over. He lay motionless. "Yep, it's a revenuer, all right," Grandpa said, and he reached down and pulled a badge from the man's inside shirt pocket. He showed it to me and added, "I can't tell you what it says, but you can bet your boots it's a lawman because they all wear them." He then proceeded to take a .38 special from each of their pockets and said, "Run as hard as you can to the mouth of the hollow and fetch old man Spaulding and his son to help me hide the still before they come to their senses. While you are doing that, I'll put the fire out and try to cool it off."

I broke into a run and didn't stop until I found Mr. Spaulding in his cornfield. I explained what had happened, and he wasted no time running to his house to get his horse. He lifted me on first, and within a few minutes we were back at the still.

Hardly a word was spoken. The revenuers continued to lay helpless on the ground, and the activity as Grandpa and Mr. Spaulding moved the still did not disturb them. When they were finished and the still had been safely hidden around the hill from its original site, Grandpa invited Mr. Spaulding down to the cabin, but Mr. Spaulding insisted on returning home.

As we arrived at the cabin and stepped on the porch, Grandpa yelled, "Elizabeth, boil a big pot of coffee and fix some extra hominy grits. Sooner or later, we are going to have visitors." He went on inside the house and deposited the pistols on a shelf in the kitchen.

It was almost dark when the revenuers made their way down to the cabin. All three came staggering through the front yard; one plopped down in Grandpa's rocker, and the other two lay down on the porch. None of the three looked very well.

Grandpa was standing in the doorway with a big smile on his face, and I hid behind Grandma Elizabeth. Old Blue was nowhere in sight.

"Well, well, just what in the world brings you fellers to this part of the country?" Grandpa chided. Before they had a chance to answer, he continued, "You know, not too many strangers ever make it in and out of here. Just where you fellers from?"

The man in the rocker, who appeared to be the leader, glanced up and said softly, "Huntington. We are federal men, you know, and we have a report that you have been making moonshine again, John." The man seemed to be trying to be as pleasant as possible under the circumstances.

Grandpa replied, "Well, I don't think there's a word of truth to that. Don't reckon you found anything that made you think contrary, did you?'' He glanced backwards at Grandma. He knew the man's reply was going to determine if he was in serious trouble.

The man hesitated, looked down at his two buddies on the floor, and slowly answered, ''No, John, we haven't found a thing.''

Grandpa, with a sigh of relief in his voice, said, ''Grandma, run in the kitchen there and get that black coffee and hominy grits on the table, and let's get these fellers straightened out.''

An hour or so later, Grandpa gave the men a half-gallon of moonshine, along with their three revolvers, and sent them on their way. Later that evening, just before we went to bed, he looked over at me and winked. ''You know, Sissie, there is still a few good strangers left in this old world.''

2

Word usually spread quickly up and down the creeks when Goodlow and Lora Fleming were going to have a corn-hoeing or a bean-stringing. Entire families came from miles around to participate in the work. Of course, there were a few who came just to flirt with the girls or to gorge themselves on chicken and dumplings. But for the most part, a corn-hoeing was a rather serious undertaking. Practically every family would have at least two corn-hoeings a year—one in the early spring when the corn first came through the ground and the blades were six or seven inches high and the second one prior to the Fourth of July. The second hoeing was called "laying it by," which meant the corn patch would not have to be attended to again until harvest time.

In an effort to break the monotony of hoeing corn, the men and women made a sport out of it. Since all the cornfields were on the sides of the hills, the fastest hoer always took the first or bottom row, called the "lead" row, so as not to rake dirt down on the unhoed rows. If the lead hoer was overtaken, he was forced to exchange rows. Thus, a person could start out in the first row and finish in the last row if overtaken by all the hoers. When the hoers approached the end of their rows, they would sprint like runners. The ones who finished first stood and yelled to the others, sometimes shouting words of encouragement and sometimes poking fun because they were so slow in finishing.

June and I were the water-carriers. We were expected to have a bucket of fresh cold water waiting at the end of each row, and I have never seen water drunk quite like the times I watched twelve or fourteen corn hoers each devour a peck bucket of water. Some drank from the dippers while others just turned the buckets to their mouths. It was actually a relief when I became of hoeing age and left the task of carrying water to my younger brother and sister.

The bean-stringings were equally exciting and perhaps even more fun because they were always followed by an old-time "hoedown." During the day, a group of five or six would go to the fields to pick the beans while another group strung the beans and broke them in preparation for canning or sewing together on long strings, which were then hung on the walls to dry. The dried beans were called "leatherbritches." I never really appreciated them myself, but my father thought there was nothing like a good "mess" of leatherbritches on a cold winter day.

When the day's work was completed, out came the fiddles, guitars, and banjos, along with several fruit jars of Ol' Twelve-Toed John's moonshine, and the frolic would commence. Such square dance tunes as "Black Mountain Rag" and "Sally in the Lowground" echoed down the hollow until nearly dawn, while the hooting, howling, and square dancing were a sight to behold. The moonshine drinking was usually reserved for the men and boys, although occasionally we girls would steal a little nip.

Some of the older people who felt the hoedowns were a little too fast for them would gather in one of the back rooms and tell ghost stories to the children until they were scared nearly to death. I heard them all. There was "Old Bloody Bones," "Old Raw Bones," and the scariest of the lot, the one about the graveyard dirt falling through the loft. According to the story, a neighbor had murdered a friend one night during a quarrel, chopped his head off with a double-bit axe, and buried him under the house. The murderer was later caught and hanged by the neck, but from that day on, graveyard dirt could be seen falling through the loft of that house. My grandma told me that all the people on the hollow used to gather there on occasion to witness the phenomenon. Around midnight a most mournful sound would come from under the floor, a sound so terrible that it "would make the hair stand straight up on the back of a cur dog." Then a few minutes later, the graveyard dirt would come falling down. It was fresh, yellow clay just like that from a newly dug grave. The men would take a ladder and climb up to the attic but could never find anything.

After a few of these stories, we would be hustled off to bed where we promptly pulled the cover over our heads and sometimes nearly suffocated. But it was better than being caught by Old Bloody Bones.

Social activities, of course, declined when school began in the fall. I attended a one-room school across the mountain from Newground Hollow on Turkey Creek. Altogether there were seventeen students from various creeks and hollows. Our teacher was "Aunt" Sally Slater, a courageous and devoted woman who came all the way from Williamson, the county seat of Mingo County, some forty miles west of Turkey Creek. During the week, she lived with a local family, returning to Williamson on the weekends. She was a handsome woman in her mid-fifties and our only contact with the world outside.

The schoolhouse was a small white rectangular structure with a small bell tower atop a high gabled roof. A large entrance door opened into a small foyer where the water bucket was stored along with the drinking glasses. A second door led into the main classroom, which had a twenty-foot ceiling. Seven oversized windows lined the left side. To the right was a narrow hallway that served as a cloakroom. A large potbellied stove sat at the back of the room. There were twenty huge desks with large tops that sloped slightly downward, and each had its own inkwell. In the front of the room to the right of Aunt Sally's desk was a long rotation bench. Each grade was called to the front of the room at various intervals and seated on the rotation bench where they would read aloud, spell, and recite poetry. While one grade was up front, the others remained in their seats and worked on their silent reading, writing, and arithmetic. Large slate blackboards covered the front of the room and extended around the right side. The advanced grades, usually sixth, seventh, and eighth, used the blackboards to do their arithmetic lessons.

Drinking water was carried from a spring around the hill from the school, and Aunt Sally put drops of chlorine in the water to purify it. Two outside toilets sat beside each other at the back of the schoolhouse. A tattered wooden fence surrounded the playground, which was worn bare of grass. A flagpole stood to the left of the front porch.

Very few of the students who attended the Turkey Creek school ever made it to high school. The nearest high school was more than thirty miles away, and in general the parents showed very little interest in urging their children to attend.

Aunt Sally did try to encourage the students to continue

their educations. She frequently took time to tell us about life in Williamson, which in those years was noted for its railroad coal storage yard, supposed to be the largest in the world. There was even a picture of the yard in our seventh-grade geography book.

At twelve years of age I had never been off Twelve Pole Creek, except for an occasional trip with my mother and father to the little towns of Kermit and Crum. On these occasions we usually got to stay for several hours so we would have the opportunity to watch the passenger trains pass along the main line of the Norfolk and Western Railroad. We would wave at the engineers, and if they weren't preoccupied with operating the trains, they would wave back.

Needless to say, I was overjoyed when Aunt Sally invited me one weekend to visit her home. We rode the Greyhound bus to Williamson that Friday evening. It was my first time ever to ride a bus, and by the time we pulled into Williamson, I realized that I was entering a new and exciting world. Never before had I seen so many people. The neon signs were flashing brightly as we turned into the station. The large railroad passenger terminal was directly across the street, and people were coming and going in all directions. Several steam engines sat near the station chugging slowly as if gasping for their last breaths. Aunt Sally held firmly to my shoulder as she hailed a taxi to take us to her home in Chattaroy, a small mining community just outside the Williamson city limits.

That evening I met several of Aunt Sally's grandchildren. All were older than I, but I took right up to them, and they seemed to like me immediately. They made plans to take me to the moving picture show in Williamson on Saturday evening following a tour of the railroad yard and the rest of the city. Aunt Sally had told me that more than six thousand people lived in Williamson. It was hard to imagine that many people in one place.

The picture show turned out to be a real shock. Although my mother had told me about movie houses and picture shows, I had somehow failed to grasp that I was not going to be seeing real live people on stage. So when Roy Rogers started chasing the crooks and shooting in my direction, I ducked behind the seat in front of me and buried my head in my lap, frightened nearly out of my wits. I couldn't understand why the girls were laughing. But when they realized that I was really frightened, they explained that it was not for real and that I would not be shot. Reluctantly, I accepted their explanation and watched the rest of the movie, but I must admit that I had a very difficult time sleeping that night. It was all too much to comprehend.

I had never paid much attention to boys before, but Aunt Sally's grandson, Glen, really caught my eye. Perhaps it was because there was so much talk about boys among Aunt Sally's granddaughters, or maybe I was just reaching the age where girls start noticing. But one thing for certain, I thought Glen was the most handsome fellow I had ever seen. He must have been about seventeen, so there was very little possibility of his ever noticing me, but it didn't keep me from thinking about him. After I went back home, I wrote him a letter and gave it to Aunt Sally to take to him. She gave me a rather peculiar look and commented that I was awfully young to be writing love letters but promised she would give it to him. I suppose she did, but Glen never answered it.

About this time, two of the boys in my class began giving me quite a bit of attention—Sam Workman, a thin, scrawny boy, and Jethro Spaulding, who was tall, muscular, and jovial. Both were fifteen years old, and neither was very interested in school. Aunt Sally had a hard time keeping them under control.

Occasionally, Aunt Sally would take her classes on a hike through the woods where she would help us observe the various types of birds and point out the different varieties of plant life. On one of these occasions, Sam suddenly grabbed my hand, pulled me from the rear of the line, and whispered, "Fannie Belle, let's slip off over here a little ways and pick some mountain tea."

"What are you wanting to do, get us in trouble with Aunt Sally? Besides, there ain't no mountain tea over here on this side of the mountain; you're just making that up," I replied, not wanting to create a stir.

Looking surprised that I had questioned his offer, he said, "Fannie Belle, do you think I'd lie to you? I hold my hand to God and hope He strikes me down with lightning if I am lying."

Sure that nobody would dare hold his hand up and swear to God about something like that and take a chance on being struck down by lightning, I believed he was telling the truth, but I was still hesitant. "Well, let's suppose there is some mountain tea where you say it is, what's Aunt Sally going to say when she misses us?" I asked. We had already fallen back some fifty feet behind the rest of the class.

"Aw, Fannie Belle, you know she ain't going to miss us at least for about thirty minutes. Besides, we'll pick enough mountain tea for everybody," he said.

I decided it would probably be all right. The kids all liked "mountain tea," as we called it, although Aunt Sally had told us it was wintergreen. Whatever its name, it certainly tasted good, so I agreed to slip off with Sam. I said, "Okay, but let's hurry; I sure don't want to get into trouble with Aunt Sally."

Sam grinned, tightened his grip on my hand, and began to ease farther back until the rest of the kids were out of sight. "Come on; it's right over here in this swag. Me and Jethro found it last year. It ain't more than a hundred yards to it,'' he said excitedly, as we hurried around a rock ledge to the site he had pointed out.

As we neared the patch of mountain tea, he turned loose of my hand and ran ahead. "See there, Fannie Belle, what did I tell you? Ain't that the purtiest patch of mountain tea you ever seen?''

I must admit it was all he had said it was. A large crooked circle of earth was covered with the shiny, dark green creeper. The berries weren't quite ripe yet, just turning a pretty pink. We began picking, first cramming our mouths full of the woody, fresh-tasting leaves and chewing on them as we picked some for the other kids. We had been there almost twenty minutes picking the tea and talking about how excited the others would be when it dawned on me that Sam should have told Aunt Sally about the tea patch so everyone could have come. I asked him, "Sam, why didn't you tell Aunt Sally about this?''

" 'Cause this is mine and Jethro's secret patch. When we found it last year, we both swore that we weren't going to tell another soul.''

"Well, you told me about it.''

"Yeah, but you're different.'' He hesitated. "You ain't going to tell Jethro, are you?''

"Of course not,'' I replied. "What do you think I am, a tattletale?''

"Well, you never know. I just thought you might have a slip of the tongue, and if you did, Jethro sure wouldn't like it. Why, he would never trust me again.''

"Don't worry, I won't tell. But look, we've been gone long enough. Besides, we've got enough for the others,'' I said as I raised up, then tripped forward.

As I stumbled, Sam grabbed me with both hands and kissed me, and we both fell to the ground, spilling our mountain tea in the process. "Sam Workman, you kissed me!'' I shouted as I jumped to my feet.

"Aw, Fannie Belle, I didn't mean nothing by it," he replied sheepishly.

"What do you mean you didn't mean nothing by it? I am going to tell Aunt Sally on you," I said.

"Never mind, Fannie Belle, I'll take care of Sam Workman right now. I seen him kiss you." It was Jethro Spaulding. He had slipped off from the class and followed us to the tea patch. Apparently he had hidden behind the big oak tree and had been watching us for a long time. John Marcum was with him.

Jethro rushed past me, grabbed Sam, and hit him a good one right under the eye. As the commotion broke out, John Marcum and I ran as hard as we could until we caught up with the rest of the class. As we reached the group, John yelled, "Hey, Aunt Sally, you had better come. Sam Workman kissed Fannie Belle, and Jethro Spaulding is giving him a good licking over it."

I turned red all over, and the kids began to laugh. Aunt Sally ran to the rear of the line and asked, "Fannie Belle, what's this all about? Where have you been?"

I replied nervously, "Well . . . uh . . .," but it was hard to find the right words.

"Come on, girl, tell me where you have been!" she demanded.

"The mountain tea patch with Sam." The kids were still laughing.

"You all quiet down," Aunt Sally said in a stern voice. "You kids stay here until I get back," she added as she took me by the arm. "Come on, Fannie Belle, show me where the boys are."

I tried to explain that we had not meant anything and that I was sorry, but Aunt Sally was upset. As we approached the tea patch, Sam and Jethro were coming up the hill towards us. Jethro had bloodied Sam's nose and blacked his eye.

"Now just look at you two!" Aunt Sally said angrily.

She stopped the two of them, broke off a hickory limb, and began to flail the daylights out of them both.

I felt sorry for the boys, but at the same time I couldn't help but feel a little flattered that they had been fighting over me. I went home that evening and thought a lot about Sam and Jethro. The kiss had been fun. I told June about it, and we talked late into the night about kissing and courting boys.

3

It was a long way to Harts Creek; the best I could figure it was about forty miles. It took me and my Grandma Fannie two days to make the trip on foot. We stopped at the head of Cub Branch the first day to spend the night with relatives.

Most of my mother's mother's folks lived on Cub Branch. In fact, that's where she met my Grandpa Dick Evans. He had been married two or three times before and had a slew of children by his other wives. According to some of the talk by the old-timers, he might just have had a bunch more by some other women. Grandpa was a champion fiddler, and everyone called him ''Fiddler Dick.''

Grandma talked about Grandpa a lot, telling me time and time again how they had met and how she fell in love with him. His death when I was only three years old had been hard for her to accept. Right after that she came to Newground Hollow and made her life with us.

It was also about this time, according to Grandma, that

she "got right with the Lord," and she became an active participant in a little church at the mouth of the hollow called the Church of Zion. She was well thought of in the community and in the church. Frequently she gave lengthy testimonials affirming her faith in the Lord, and she often gave the "altar call," pleading with the sinners to give their souls to God. Had she been a man, I am sure she would have been a preacher. But women preachers were not permitted in her church, and people on the creek generally frowned upon the idea, besides. According to them, there simply wasn't any scripture that gave a woman the right to preach. On those rare occasions when a woman felt she had been "called by the Lord to preach," it was considered an act of the Devil, and women preachers were denied fellowship in most of the churches.

Grandma Fannie had been a great influence on my mother, who was also a devout Christian. My father, Goodlow, was a little different. He believed in God but had become somewhat disillusioned with religion during "Hoover's Depression." On many occasions I had heard him down on his knees praying for God to give his family some relief. He was unemployed for eight years and usually was able to earn only eight or ten dollars a month doing odd jobs. Prior to the Depression, he had worked as a coal miner, and it was only after World War II broke out that he was able to return to work. When Grandma encouraged my father to go to church, he always reminded her that he hadn't received much help from God during Hoover's Depression when he needed it most, and he figured He wasn't going to look any more favorably upon him now. Grandma expressed concern about my father's attitude but always added that she reckoned the Lord would take care of the matter in His own time.

It was the annual, Evans Memorial Service that brought about our trek to Harts. To help me get ready for it, Grandma Fannie had spent weeks teaching me how to sew.

Except for learning to cook, she said it was the most important thing a young girl could learn to do. Together we made a beautiful dress from cotton print I had bought from a pack peddler. I had earned the money for the material by picking blackberries and selling them to the folks on Twelve Pole Creek for fifteen cents a peck. Grandma said I would have the prettiest dress at the reunion.

Entire families came from miles around to attend the all-day preaching with dinner on the ground. The meeting was held in the cemetery, where workers had built a pulpit and platform from rough-sawn oak. The benches for the worshipers were also oak boards resting on blocks of wood. A large, bench-like table had been constructed in an oak grove a few hundred feet from the cemetery. The table was fifty or sixty feet long and large enough to accommodate many, many lard cans of chicken and dumplings, and ham, mutton, fried chicken, apple pies, and trays of banana pudding.

It was at this meeting that I met Wes Evans, a tall, handsome mountain boy who was seventeen or eighteen years old. I had been sitting on a bench behind him and couldn't help but be impressed with his dark, wavy hair. When the services broke for dinner, he looked back at me with a broad grin on his face and said, "Boy, am I glad that preaching is over. I am starved to death!"

"Me, too," I replied.

As we eased our way towards the end of the bench, to my delight he continued the conversation. "Say, where are you from?" he inquired.

"Newground Hollow, up in Wayne County. It's right on the Mingo County line. That was my grandma making the altar call just after the last preacher."

"Is that a fact? She's sure a serious-talking woman, and she's got a powerful voice to go with it."

"Yeah, I guess she does all right," I said.

"Say, purty thing, what's your name?"

I turned red. I had never had a boy refer to me as "purty thing." Bashfully, I replied, "Fannie Belle Fleming."

"Well, Fannie Belle, how about you and me getting us a big plate of chicken and dumplings and some banana pudding and slip off away from the crowd where we can have us a picnic?" he invited.

"Well, I guess that would be all right, but I had better tell Grandma so she won't be looking for me. If you'll wait here, I'll be right back."

He nodded, and I rushed up to the pulpit where Grandma Fannie was engaging a preacher in a discussion of the scripture. As soon as I had a chance to interrupt her discussion, I told her what I was going to do. She said it would be all right but wanted me to point out the young man. I pointed him out, then ran back to where Wes was waiting.

We hurried through the line, helping ourselves to a little of everything. Then I followed Wes around the mountain-side until we were a good distance from the crowd and found a flat rock that made an ideal picnic spot.

Within a few minutes, Wes had devoured his food, leaving me only about half finished. I was so nervous that I had lost most of my appetite anyway.

"How old are you, Fannie Belle?" he inquired.

"Fifteen," I lied. I was afraid he would think I was too young to pay any more attention to if I admitted I was only thirteen. Anyway, I was almost fourteen, and that was getting pretty old. Grandma Fannie had married when she was fourteen. Besides, I could easily pass for fifteen or sixteen.

"Have you got a boy back home?" he questioned.

"Not any special one," I replied. "There is one boy who likes me an awful lot."

He interrupted. "I bet every boy around there likes you."

I blushed again and waited to see what else he was

going to say. Never before had I met such an outspoken boy, and I was at a loss for words.

"You sure are a purty thing. I just haven't seen too many red-headed girls that I could go for, but that sure ain't the case with you." He reached over and pulled me close to him and ran his fingers through my hair.

"Wes, I think we had better go. I told Grandma that I wouldn't be gone long." I didn't really want to leave, but I was afraid to stay.

"Don't worry, we haven't been gone that long," he assured me. Then he pulled me tighter to him and kissed me.

I was trembling with excitement, but after a few minutes I sensed that things were about to get out of control. Pulling back, I said, "I like you, Wes, but I've got to go now or Grandma will get worried."

Before the weekend was over, Wes and I managed to see each other several times. Whenever we had a chance, we slipped away from the crowd. On Sunday night, church services were held at a private home, and we hid behind a rose bush. That night Wes had me so excited that I nearly gave in to his advances. But just as he attempted to unbutton my blouse, I pulled away. I knew it was then or never. I thought about all the other girls on the hollow who had failed to break away. I certainly didn't want to wind up having to get married.

Before we left the next day, I promised Wes that I would write him. As we walked back to Newground Hollow, I told Grandma Fannie about him and asked what she thought about my inviting Wes to visit. She said she saw no problem with it but indicated that my father might not be so agreeable.

Grandma had married when she was only fourteen, and back in the hills most of the girls still married around the age of sixteen. I had blossomed into full womanhood by the time I was thirteen and had become aware that a lot of the boys were looking me over. Wes was the first who had attempted to be serious with me, however. I thought about him a lot and later wrote him a couple of letters, but the romance was short-lived. The distance between Newground Hollow and Harts Creek was just too far.

Occasionally violence flared on Twelve Pole Creek. Everyone carried a gun, and sometimes neighbors killed each other. Frequently it was just a matter of each man refusing to back down in an argument. I never figured it all out. It made no sense to me. The mountain people called it pride.

When there was a death, Grandma Fannie was often called to comfort the family, and I sometimes traveled with her. A wake would be held, and all the relatives and neighbors would come to sit up with the dead for two or three days before the burial.

I recall one wake for a man who was killed by his neighbor. One of the man's cows had broken into the neighbor's corn patch, and the neighbor gunned him down with a twelve-gauge shotgun. The victim didn't have a chance.

The body was sent to Logan, a town thirty miles away, for embalming. When it was brought back home, everyone gathered in to see how good a job the undertaker had done fixing him up. The casket was set up in the living room with several wreaths of flowers placed alongside. Most of the people who came brought food and drinks, for the wake would last for two nights. I spent most of that first evening out on the front porch while Grandma was inside consoling the family.

Old Jeb Collins, who lived about six miles from Newground Hollow, never missed a wake or a funeral. It was about dusk when he came across the creek on the foot log and, wearing a solemn look on his face, made his way up the steps. Some of the men were standing with their feet propped up on the porch bannister, chewing tobacco and musing about how the shooting incident had taken place. Old Jeb began shaking hands with everyone and finally worked his way over to where I was sitting. Recognizing me, he asked, "Is Goodlow here?"

"No," I replied in a half whisper, "he's planning on coming down later." Somehow it didn't seem polite to talk out loud with the corpse in the living room.

Jeb turned to one of the older neighbors and asked, "How does he look?"

"I don't know, Jeb. They ain't going to open the casket until the older boy gets here around ten o'clock."

Jeb looked a little disappointed that he was going to have to wait that long. He turned to another neighbor and said, "I'll bet you they have him fixed up nice."

The neighbor replied, "Yeah, I bet they do, too. That undertaker Jason knows what he's doing. I seen him take and put back a feller's head that had been blown halfway off. He took a picture and some wax, and you couldn't tell where he had patched him up."

Every now and then, some adult would yell at the children who were playing boisterously in the yard. The food had been set out on the table already, and there was a steady stream in and out of the kitchen.

An older woman who had known the victim came out on the porch and sat in the swing beside me. She was half crying, "I'll tell you, there was not a better man anywhere. I sometimes don't understand why the Lord lets things like this happen."

She had hardly finished the sentence when someone responded, "It's just the Lord's will. When He gets ready to take you out of this old world, there ain't a thing you can do about it. It was just his time to go."

At intervals, members of the victim's family would cry out, especially when they walked into the living room where the casket sat. Each time this happened, silence would fall over the crowd until the crying stopped.

When the oldest son arrived, the casket was opened, and there was an emotional outburst from the members of the immediate family. Finally, the widow was taken to another room, and the parade past the coffin began. Some of the visitors still carried their sandwiches as they viewed the corpse.

Old Jeb was one of the first to take a look. He pulled his handkerchief from his rear pocket and wiped his eyes. He stood over the corpse for several minutes, occasionally shaking his head as if in disbelief.

The body had been dressed in a dark blue suit with the hair neatly combed and hands folded on the chest. Finally, Jeb and several of the first viewers made their way back to the front porch and began to discuss the corpse.

Jeb was the first to comment, "I'll tell you, that undertaker sure enough did a good job. Why, he looks like he is just asleep."

Another man chimed in, "Yeah, you can't even tell where he was shot. I was talking to a fellow who helped carry him to the ambulance. Said his right eyeball was clean out on his cheekbone and most of his nose was gone. I looked especially close, and I couldn't tell a thing."

"Yeah, he sure is natural-looking," a woman whispered.

About thirty minutes later, one of the local ministers started preaching in the front room. He told all the sinners that they should take heed, that no one ever knows when the good Lord is going to take them away. Occasionally there would be an amen from across the room.

The ministers always managed to say some good things about the deceased, and, of course, everyone always agreed, regardless of how bad the person had been. I guess it made the families feel better to think their loved ones would go to heaven rather than to hell. Grandma, like the ministers, had very vivid descriptions of heaven and hell. Heaven, she said, was a place of total happiness, where the streets were paved with gold. Hell was nothing but eternal fire and brimstone.

Like everyone else, I couldn't stand the thought of going to hell and worried about it quite a bit.

4

For lack of other activities, I spent a second year in the eighth grade at Aunt Sally's school. That year my sister June, who was sixteen, slipped off and married Luther Spaulding, a young coal miner from Buffalo Creek in neighboring Logan County, some forty miles from Newground Hollow. By the time my second eighth grade had ended, I too was becoming restless and bored with life in Newground Hollow and was looking for a way to get out. But every time the subject was mentioned, my father sternly objected. He insisted that I was too young to leave home, that it was just too easy for a young girl to get herself in trouble. He had tended to become more protective of me after June's marriage. Terribly disappointed that she had chosen to run away at such a tender age, he vowed that it would not happen again in his family.

I guess, too, my father was afraid I might turn out like my Aunt Mabel. She had left home at an early age in circumstances nobody talked about much, and eventually she went into business near Williamson. "Mabel's Place"

43

was one of the most notorious in the country. Aunt Mabel knew all the politicians, so when she peddled moonshine by the drink, they always turned their heads. As far as I know, she was never arrested or fined for her illicit business, but her reputation as a "bootlegger" spread far and near.

Soon after her marriage, June suffered a miscarriage and was in very poor health for a while. Luther had to work every day and was unable to care for her, so one afternoon he came to see if I could go live with them until June recovered. My mother aptly agreed that I should go, and I packed my clothing and such other belongings as I thought I would need and left with Luther that same day.

As soon as June regained her health, I took a job as a waitress at the Kistler Grill, a beer hall and poolroom combination. It was a violation of the law for anyone under eighteen to serve beer, but at fourteen my bust was already a size 36-C. I could pass for eighteen, and the owner of the Grill did not bother to ask my age when I applied for the job.

Buffalo Creek at that time was a bustling, coal-mining community; the entire valley was dotted with mining camps. The Kistler Grill was visited regularly by the coal miners as they changed shifts. Only on rare occasions would a female enter the place. Keeping it clean was a terrible job. The miners would come in after a shift's work with black coal dust covering their hard hats and hard-toed boots and would sometimes sit and drink beer for hours. Occasionally, there would be a barroom ruckus, and these sometimes resulted in serious facial lacerations for the people hit by broken beer bottles. When this happened, I ducked down behind the bar and stayed there until it was all over. Many of the young coal miners made passes at me, but I ignored them.

The Kistler Grill also served as a bus stop for the Consolidated Bus Lines. Cliff Titus, a driver for the line, would always take time out to have a cup of coffee and engage in some small talk. He had been married but claimed that he and his wife just couldn't make it, so they were divorced. His bus run was local, serving mainly the mining communities on Buffalo Creek, but he did have one evening run that took him to Henlawson about forty miles away.

On several occasions, Cliff told me that he could get me a good job at a drive-in restaurant that had just opened up near Logan. It was called the Outside Inn. I didn't take his offer seriously until my sister and her husband began fighting, sometimes as often as once a week. Each time this happened, Luther beat June. The situation was one I could not understand, for my mother and father had never quarreled, much less fought physically, and I could not stand the violence. Finally, I decided to take Cliff up on his offer, and he arranged an interview with the owner, Harriet. Since the Outside Inn also sold beer, I lied again about my age and was hired.

The restaurant was located on a main highway, and it gave me an opportunity to meet a lot of people. I lived with Harriet. Cliff frequently came by in the evenings when he was off from work, and I would stand by his car and talk when I wasn't busy. The young boys who frequented the restaurant were always making passes or asking for a date. I would usually lead them on, as it would often pay off with a larger tip. It also got me in trouble one evening.

It was nearing midnight, and the car with the three young men had been on the curb for almost two hours. Each boy had drunk five or six beers, and all of them were beginning to feel their oats a little. Ultimately, they moved their car to the far end of the curb to a dark area that was rather isolated from the drive-in. When I went out to serve the next round, the boy who had been sitting in the back seat was standing outside the car. Just as I placed the tray on the window and said that would be sixty cents, he grabbed me and threw me into the back seat. The driver handed the other boy the beers, and the car sped away as fast as possible. I kicked, screamed, and bit the boy's hands, but he overpowered me and held me face down in the back seat. I pleaded with them to take me back, but the driver yelled, "Shut up, goddammit, or we'll beat the hell out of you!"

As I cried louder, the boy who was holding me down slapped me hard, and I sobbed that I would be quiet. He said, "Now I am going to let you up, but so help me God, if you scream again, I am going to knock the hell out of you and roll your ass out into the ditch."

I nodded my head and managed to hold my cries to an occasional sob as he gradually released the pressure on my arms and neck. I sat up slowly in the seat, desperately trying to figure out what to do.

The car sped on through the town of Logan and turned left on U.S. Route 119 towards Charleston, the state capital, which was about seventy-five miles away. By this time, I had got my wits back but was still terribly frightened. The boys up front had finished their beers and had thrown the bottles out the window and up into the air behind the car.

"What's your name, honey?" the driver asked. He appeared to be in his early twenties. The one who had subdued me was about the same age, the other somewhat younger.

Afraid not to answer, I said, "Fannie Belle Fleming."

"Well, I ain't telling you mine, not just yet," he chortled.

The young man in the back reached down and put his fingers on my leg. I immediately seized his hand to prevent him from moving it farther, but did not try to force him to remove it for fear he would slap me again.

The driver continued, "Fannie, have you ever had any

before? Surely a girl as pretty as you hasn't been going to waste, have you?''

When I did not respond, he kept talking. The younger boy would occasionally glance back and grin.

''Little Boy here in the front ain't never had any. Claims he has, but we know better. Anyway, we'll be able to tell if he's been lying pretty soon now. A man can always tell when a fellow has had a little before and when he ain't, and I'm betting he ain't.'' He reached over and slapped the younger boy on the shoulder and let out with a loud yell.

The boy in the back leaned over and whispered, ''I didn't mean to hurt you, baby. You all right? Now you just cooperate a little and enjoy yourself, and everything will be just fine.''

''Please don't hurt me, please,'' I begged.

Occasionally we met another car, probably coal miners returning from their midnight shift. I thought about trying to jump from the car but feared that would kill me for sure. The boy in the back seat continued to try to run his hand up under my dress.

Little Boy, as the driver called him, opened the glove compartment, took out a pint of liquor, had a big drink, and passed it back to the boy in the back. He released my leg as he reached for the bottle. Then wiping the mouth of the bottle, he turned it to his lips and drank all he could hold in his mouth before swallowing in one huge gulp. He opened his mouth and took in a deep breath of air and shouted, ''That goddamn shit is hot!'' Then he held the bottle to my lips and said, ''Here, baby, take a drink. It will loosen you up.''

Hoping to satisfy him, I swallowed just enough to let him know that I had taken a drink.

As the car sped on towards Charleston, the driver questioned, ''Who is going to be first?''

''I am,'' the boy in the back replied.

I began to sob again, and the driver yelled, "Shut up, goddammit! You can sob when everything is over with. I'll bet this won't be your first time anyway. A set of knockers like you've got have to be exercised a little, or they wouldn't grow that big, would they, Little Boy?" Again he reached over and slapped Little Boy on the shoulder and whooped.

"I know," he continued, "we'll let Little Boy go first since he claims he's all experienced. We'll just let him put the make on her."

The headlights of the car focused on a sign that read, "You are now entering the property of Island Creek Coal Company for the next fourteen miles." The driver slowed the car to a halt beside it. "I've got to take a piss," he said. "You guys don't let her out." Each took his turn, and there was no way for me to escape.

"What about you, Fannie Belle, you need to go?" I shook my head no.

As the driver started the car again, he mumbled, "We'll take her atop of Blair Mountain. I know a place there where we can pull completely off the highway. I've used that spot before."

"Yeah," replied the boy beside me, "that's a good place. If she causes us any trouble, we'll take her and put her in a sinkhole and cover her with leaves."

Within a few minutes we had driven to the top of Blair Mountain. I remembered one of the coal miners at the Kistler Grill telling about the Battle of Blair Mountain in the twenties. Federal troops had been sent in to put down a rebellion that broke out during attempts to organize the United Mine Workers Union. Blair Mountain was where the two sides met and fought for two days before the federal troops finally routed the coal miners. Then I thought how strange it was to remember that story at such a time.

The car pulled slowly off the highway onto a side road

and came to a stop. "Okay, Little Boy, get back there and do your thing."

The older boys got out of the car, and the young one crawled over the back of the seat. He was all over me before I knew what was happening. He was breathing terribly fast and was pawing at my breasts.

I was frightened nearly out of my wits. Finally, I pushed him back and said, "Take it easy. I've got to go to the bathroom."

He gave me a puzzled look and said, "All right, but I'm going with you."

As we got out of the car, one of the other boys asked, "Where in the hell you taking her, Little Boy?"

"She's got to go, man. It's okay. I'm going with her."

"Just keep an eye on her and hurry up, dammit!"

We walked about fifty feet from the parked car. It was pitch dark. He still held on to my arm.

"Well, what are you waiting on? Go ahead!" he demanded.

"Would you please turn your head?" I pleaded.

As he let loose of my arm, I leaped forward and ran around the hill as fast as I could go. I ran through the underbrush and patches of briars, but they did not slow my pace. I heard him shout to the other boys, "She's getting away! She's getting away!"

"Goddammit, Little Boy, you son of a bitch, catch her!" All three were giving chase and were close on my trail.

I had been running for ten or fifteen minutes and was ready to collapse when I decided to climb a tall pine tree. It took all the strength I could muster, but within a few seconds I was halfway up the tree and completely hidden. I could hear the boys searching for me down below.

One of them yelled out, "He-ey, Fannie Belle, come on back. We won't hurt you. We'll take you home."

I remained silent. As the wind blew through the trees, I thought about my mother and father and could visualize our cabin on Newground Hollow. I started sobbing again but not loud enough for the boys to hear.

"He-ey, Fannie Belle, come on out of there or a big bear will get you. You don't want to be eaten up by a bear, now do you?" The voice echoed down the valley. I shut my eyes and held on firmly to the tree. My dress had been torn down the front, and I could feel the blood from the scratches as I wiped my face. I thought of Grandma Fannie and whispered a prayer to God to help me.

Finally, there were no more yells from the boys. An hour passed, then two. Only the country night sounds could be heard. A screech owl hooted from the other side of the mountain, and had it not been for my growing up in the woods around Newground Hollow, the unearthly, lonely call would have scared me. I dared not move until daylight.

At last I began to hear the sound of cars climbing Blair Mountain and knew it was coal miners going to work. I skinned down the tree and made my way up the side of the mountain to the road in hopes of catching a ride back to Logan where I could get Harriet to call the police.

Not knowing for certain whether the boys had really left the area, I hid behind a clump of bushes at the road's edge. In the distance I could hear a huge truck coming up the mountain. Just as the truck rounded the curve, I jumped in front of it and began waving both hands. The driver brought the truck to a stop, leaned over and opened the door, and pulled me inside.

"My God, girl, what in the world has happened to you?" he asked with a frightened expression on his face.

I could not answer but buried my head in my lap and began to cry. He placed his arm on my shoulder and said, "Here, now, relax. Let me help you." He pulled a big red bandanna handkerchief from his pocket and began wiping my face.

When I regained some composure, I explained to him

what had happened. He shook his head in disbelief. He was a kind man, probably in his early forties. Even though it was off his route, he agreed to take me directly to the Outside Inn, where Harriet would be doing the morning work.

It was nearing eight o'clock when we pulled up to the Inn. I remained hidden inside the truck, for I looked a mess with all the scratches and with my dress practically torn off, but I called out for Harriet. She came to the truck and opened the door. "My God, Fannie, what has happened? Tell me, child, what has happened to you?"

I grabbed her and began to cry. She held me close and said, "It's all right. You're safe."

After I had calmed down, Harriet pulled her car up right beside the truck, and I got in without any of the people around noticing. I thanked the truck driver. He grinned and winked without saying anything.

On the way to Harriet's house, I suggested that we should call the police and asked her if she knew the three boys. She obviously did but refused to tell me their names and said that it would be better if I never knew. She did tell me that one of them was the son of a prominent politician in the county and that it would only cause her trouble if she pressed the matter. Besides, I had finally confessed to her a month earlier that I was not eighteen, and she had not fired me. She was concerned now that the state police would close her down if they investigated the matter and discovered that I was under age and selling beer. By the time we arrived at her house, she had convinced me that it would be better to remain silent about the attempted rape.

Three or four days later, I went back to work. Cliff came by and wanted to know where I had been. I reluctantly told him what had happened, and he became furious. Harriet also refused to tell him the names of the boys.

Cliff had been extremely nice to me, and we began seeing each other on a regular basis. Usually we would take some chicken or sandwiches from the drive-in after I finished work and sit by the river, eating and talking. One evening he made a pass at me and, when I pulled away, became very angry. He pulled the ticket puncher he always wore, on and off the bus, from his belt and hit me across the leg, cursing and calling me names.

"You bitch!" he cried, "you let them boys do it to you and when I touch you, you pull away. What do you think I am, some sort of fool?"

I was shocked and hurt by his behavior. He had always been so kind and gentle that I could not understand this sudden change. I asked him to take me home.

"You're damn right, I'll take you home, and it will be the last time you will ever ride my car. You damn women are all alike!" He jumped to his feet and ran towards his car. We did not speak at all on the way to Harriet's house, and I got out immediately when he stopped the car.

Later Cliff came back to the drive-in and tried to apologize, but I wouldn't talk to him. In his frustration he shouted, "I'll have you before it's over with! You just wait and see." He then backed his car onto the highway. As he accelerated, the tires squealed and gravel flew in all directions.

During the next few weeks, working at the drive-in became unbearable. Several of the young men and boys began to tease me about my experience at Blair Mountain. How the news spread was beyond me, but the more people talked about it, the more distorted the story became. The whispering behind my back and the leers and wisecracks to my face finally got so bad that I decided to leave the area. I recalled a salesman telling me about his daughter working in Washington, D.C., as a waitress. She had indicated to him that there were plenty of jobs available there. I had saved practically all the money I had earned working for Harriet and had more than enough to buy a bus ticket and pay a month's rent on an apartment.

At first Harriet did not believe me when I told her I was quitting to go to D.C. She argued that a girl my age was not ready for the big city, that men would take advantage of me, that it would all turn out bad, and that only grief and heartbreak awaited. She tried to convince me that I should stay and go on working for her. But it was all to no avail. I had already made up my mind. I was moving on.

5

The day I left West Virginia, I worked the morning shift at the drive-in and bid Harriet farewell about three o'clock in the afternoon. I hitched a ride into Logan with a salesman who had just finished having a late lunch.

The bus station in Logan was a beehive of activity. Besides serving as the terminal for Consolidated Bus Lines, it also was the terminal for all the local buses and so was always crowded with coal miners returning from work, housewives with their shopping bags, and old people who came down from the hollows to visit the social security office or a doctor in town. The station also housed five or six small shops, a poolhall, and a restaurant and beer hall.

The bus to D.C. was scheduled to depart at 4:30 P.M. and to arrive at 6:50 A.M. the next day. I had purchased my ticket early and was just standing around waiting for the bus to be announced. I don't think I had really given much thought to what I was doing there that day or where I was going until the announcer called over the public address system, "May I have your attention. Bus number

413 is now boarding for Washington, D.C., and all points in between at gate four. All aboard, please.''

Suddenly there were butterflies in my stomach, and I began to have second thoughts. What would my mother and father say when they found out I had left the state? It would be a week or two before they would know, I reasoned. Harriet would eventually write my mother, but by that time I could write from D.C. and explain everything. If all worked out all right, I knew my mother would understand.

My legs shook a little as I stepped into the bus. The driver punched my ticket, mumbled something about D.C., and smiled. Several other people were already on the bus, fanning themselves and wiping perspiration. It was a hot, muggy day. I chose a seat about halfway back in the bus next to an open window. A young marine with his duffel bag was slouched down sleeping in a seat opposite mine.

We were four hours reaching the West Virginia line, and it was almost midnight when the bus driver announced that we were approaching Roanoke, Virginia. There would be an hour layover, time for a sandwich and a coke. It was here that the young marine, Joe, introduced himself. He explained that he was on his way back to base at Quantico, Virginia. He wanted to know where I was from and where I was going. When I told him I was on my way to find work in D.C., he gave me his phone number at the base and said to call him when I got settled, and we could go to a movie. We continued our conversation on the bus until at last I fell asleep.

Joe nudged me lightly on the shoulder when we approached the outskirts of D.C. It startled me, and I shook my head, trying to remember where I was. Smiling, he leaned down and said, ''I thought you would want to take a look at the scenery since you haven't been here before.

Besides, we will be in the middle of D.C. in another thirty minutes.''

When I heard Joe mention D.C., all the drowsiness and fatigue of having slept curled up in a bus seat for several hours immediately disappeared. I hurriedly combed my hair and began fixing my face.

"You should get yourself a newspaper as soon as we get in D.C., and with luck you should find a room and a job under the classified section," Joe said as I touched up my lips.

"Do you think I will have any difficulty getting a job?" I asked.

"No, the paper is always full of want ads for waitresses," Joe answered reassuringly. "If I had time, I would hang around and help you, but I am past due at the base now."

I thanked him for his kindness and assured him that I would give him a call as soon as possible. Within minutes, I could see in the distance the Washington Monument. It was just like the picture on the calendar that hung in Old Man Marcum's store back on Twelve Pole Creek. I was terribly excited, and my heart was pounding at a furious pace. It was difficult to grasp the size of the city, especially when all I had to compare it with were Williamson and Logan. Joe began pointing out other monuments and important buildings as we approached the business district.

Once inside the bus station, I followed Joe's advice and purchased a newspaper and checked the classified section. On my first call I was able to rent a room for seven dollars a week. It was only two blocks from the bus station, so I carried all my belongings and walked there rather than take a taxi.

I rang the doorbell, and an elderly man answered. I explained, "I'm the girl who just called about the room."

"Oh, yes. Won't you come in, please. The room is on

the third floor. No drinking, no partying. We run a respectable rooming house. Any violation of the rules, and out you go," he said firmly.

"Yes, sir. I don't do either."

"I'll need you to sign the register," he said as he helped me with my luggage. "Where you from?"

"West Virginia," I replied, hoping that would satisfy his curiosity. I was sure that he had never heard of Twelve Pole Creek and that I would have difficulty attempting to explain where it was.

"Yes, indeed, that's a fine state. Got a friend up here from West Virginia, from Clarksburg," he continued as he laid a form on the desk for me to sign. "He's a taxi driver. Come here during the war. Do you know Clarksburg very well?"

"No, sir. I am from the southern part of the state, and I guess Clarksburg must be somewhere else 'cause I've never heard of it," I replied.

"Here's the key, number 303. Turn right at the top of the stairs. And that will be seven dollars in advance."

I gave him the seven dollars and climbed the stairs to my room. It was tiny but clean and neat. After unpacking my luggage, I searched the paper once again and underlined several places to call about a job. My first call was to the Mayflower Donut Shop on F Street. The man who answered the phone wanted to know when I could come in for an interview; when I told him immediately, he set it up for one o'clock.

Although the Donut Shop was only a few blocks away, this time I caught a cab for fear I would get lost if I walked. The man had explained how to get there, but it all seemed confusing. I hoped he would not question my age or require a birth certificate, for I had learned from Harriet that you really were supposed to be eighteen to work even where beer was not sold.

I told the manager of my experience as a waitress, and

he seemed to be satisfied that I could do the job. He did ask my age but did not question me further when I told him eighteen. He wanted me to start the following morning.

That night I wrote my mother and father a rather lengthy letter explaining that I had not really run away but had only come to D.C. to work. I described in detail all that I had seen coming into D.C. on the bus, how big the city was, my new job at the Donut Shop, and finally my room, and how I had kitchen privileges so I could cook up some good food for myself and not have to spend half of what I earned eating out. I asked them not to worry and promised faithfully that I would write often.

Working at the Donut Shop was enjoyable and certainly much easier than working on the curb at Harriet's drive-in. I began to develop new confidence and actually looked forward to the daily routine. People were nice, and it soon got so I knew some of the regulars to talk to.

After a week or so, I called Joe. He seemed excited to hear from me but admitted that he hadn't really expected me to call. We arranged to go to a movie that same evening. Joe was fun to be with, and during the following couple of months we spent quite a few evenings together. Occasionally, we double-dated with Joe's friend, Bill Young, and his girlfriend. One night Joe told me about moving off the base into an apartment with his sister Audrey. He didn't tell me the address, but I noticed it on a letter he accidentally dropped and I picked up.

On Joe's twenty-second birthday, I decided to surprise him with a birthday cake. I spent most of the late afternoon after I got off work mixing and baking and icing a big yellow cake with chocolate icing, and it was nearing seven o'clock when I arrived by taxi at Joe's apartment. When I rang the doorbell, a beautiful young girl answered and introduced herself as Audrey. I told her that I was

Belle Fleming and that I wanted to surprise Joe on his birthday with a home-baked cake.

"Oh, Joe has told me about you. You're the girl he met on the bus and advised about how to get a job. Come in. He and Bill stepped out a few minutes to get a beer. Said they would be right back." She took the cake to the kitchen table, complimenting me on how pretty it looked.

"I recognized you from the picture Joe showed me," I said as I followed her into the kitchen.

"It is real nice of you to do this for Joe. I am sure he will be thrilled."

"It was no trouble," I said, and I meant it. It had been very satisfying to do something for Joe, and as I had worked in the old-fashioned, rooming-house kitchen, it had occurred to me that I might be falling in love with him.

For the next twenty minutes, Audrey and I sat at the kitchen table and engaged in small talk. She talked a lot about how much she and Joe enjoyed the D.C. area. She was still talking when the boys came back.

As Joe stepped through the door, I ran and grabbed him, embracing and kissing him all in one motion. He stood stock still as I said, "Happy birthday!" There was no reply.

"What's the matter? Have I done something wrong?" I asked bewildered.

He was pale. He looked at me, then at Audrey. Finally, he blurted, "What are you doing here? How did you find this apartment?"

I explained about seeing his address on the letter he had dropped. I could not understand his behavior. Everything I said seemed to make him more nervous. "But your sister Audrey . . ." I tried again.

"What do you mean 'sister'?" Audrey asked. Her voice was suddenly icy.

I was totally dumbfounded. "You are Joe's sister, aren't you?"

"I am his wife! I am his wife!" she screamed.

Joe had been lying to me all along. He was married. Audrey was his wife. Heartbroken, I ran from the apartment. Way down the hall I could hear Audrey shouting, "Joe, you dirty son of a bitch, how could you do this to me?"

I walked in the direction of my rooming house with tears running down my face. I was both hurt and angry. I walked and walked and walked. It was near midnight when I finally got to my room, and I cried myself to sleep.

A week or so later, Joe came into the Donut Shop and told me that he had intended all along to tell me the truth about Audrey but hadn't for fear that I wouldn't go out with him. He wanted to take me to a movie and said that he would get a divorce in a few months if I would trust him. I told him to forget it, that I didn't want to see hide nor hair of him again. He immediately got out of his seat and stalked out the front door without uttering another word in his defense, and I never saw him again.

Now instead of going to the movies with Joe, I spent most of my free time window-shopping. I had never seen so many beautiful clothes in all my life. When I was home in Newground Hollow, I had spent hours thumbing through the Sears Roebuck catalog, looking at all the dresses and shoes and imagining how I would look all dressed up in those fancy store clothes. Now I had a chance to walk from store to store and see the same things right in front of me. I couldn't get up enough nerve to go inside where I could get a better look or have a chance to touch everything. Besides, I hadn't been able to save enough money to buy anything new.

On occasion I walked past the White House. I couldn't believe how big and pretty it was. How anyone could live in a house that big was beyond my imagination. I also visited the Washington Monument and the Jefferson and the Lincoln Memorial. Each time I visited one of these important places, I would write and describe it to my mother and send her a picture postcard. She wrote back and told me how much everyone missed me and how lucky I was to have the opportunity to see all these nice things and meet new people. I didn't tell her about all the times I got lost and had to ask for directions to find my room.

One morning a very tall, burly man I had never seen before came into the Donut Shop and asked whether I had ever been in show business. He introduced himself as Red Snyder and went on to explain that he had a horse act at a place called the Quonset Hut on the outskirts of the city and that he was always looking for new talent.

At first I thought he was kidding me, but as he continued the conversation I realized that he was serious. I explained that I had been in D.C. for only four months and had no experience in show business, but he continued to pursue the subject during my breaks between customers. When I told him that the only talent I had was picking the guitar and playing the harmonica, his eyes lit up, and he asked, "Would you come over to my apartment for an audition when you get off from work?"

"Are you serious? Me in show business?" I questioned.

"Yes indeed! I am dead serious," he replied.

He was dressed in a pair of cowboy boots, a Western hat and shirt, and a pair of black pants with a red stripe that almost matched the color of his hair. He appeared to be about six feet six inches tall, in his early fifties, and he must have weighed nearly three hundred pounds. When he paid his bill, he scribbled down his address and asked me to meet him at his apartment as soon as I got off work. He added that he would have Johnny Wise, his cowboy singer, there also and walked out the door.

The rest of the day at the Donut Shop was a struggle. I

could not get my mind off the scheduled audition and found myself daydreaming about being in show business. Still, I was not quite certain whether Red Snyder was authentic or just putting me on for other reasons. To make sure, I called the Quonset Hut and asked for Red Snyder. The girl who answered the phone said that Mr. Snyder would not be available until eight o'clock that night, and I congratulated myself that his offer had been legitimate.

Immediately after work, I caught a cab, went to the address he had given me, and took the elevator to the seventh floor. Mr. Snyder answered the door, and when I went inside, he introduced me to Johnny Wise. Wise grunted a hello. He, too, was dressed in a cowboy outfit like Mr. Snyder's.

"Isn't she a jewel, Johnny? Just look at her! She'll fit right into your act," Snyder said as I stood on display in the center of the room.

"Okay, let's see if she has any talent to go along with her looks," Wise said and handed me his guitar.

I nervously played two or three tunes I had learned back home. Red Snyder smiled, and Johnny Wise stared past me without expression.

As I finished the last tune, Snyder clapped his hands and said, "They will love her at the Quonset Hut. You can start tomorrow night, and I'll give you fifty dollars for the weekend."

"Oh, thank you, Mr. Snyder. I can't believe it! Me in show business! Wait until my mother finds out about this. I just can't believe it!" I said, jumping for joy.

The following evening after I got off from work at the Donut Shop, I met Mr. Snyder at a costume shop, and he bought me a cowgirl outfit. The blouse was selected for its low neckline.

I met Johnny Wise at the Quonset Hut an hour before show time to rehearse two or three songs. He was very unpleasant to work with and offered me no encouragement whatsoever. It was plain that he resented me and had from the moment we were introduced.

Mr. Snyder came to the dressing room just before show time and said that he was going to have me introduced as Starr Blaze. To me the name didn't have quite the right "ring." I suggested that we reverse it to Blaze Starr. Mr. Snyder didn't like it, and he didn't seem to like my making suggestions, either, but I was adamant, and I coaxed a little, and he finally agreed.

There was a fairly large crowd that night, and, knowing that I would soon be facing them, I was scared out of my wits. Then the master of ceremonies was introducing me as "Blaze Starr, the singing cowgirl from Texas" and there was a burst of applause as Johnny and I walked to the front of the stage and immediate laughter as I twisted myself between the guitar and its strap. There were also a few whistles from the back. Johnny and I went through two of the songs we had rehearsed, to loud applause each time. I bowed and left the stage, and Johnny sang two more songs before he brought the horse on stage to do its tricks.

Mr. Snyder was watching from the rear of the stage, and as I walked off he said, "Great job. They loved you!" He put his arm around me and hugged me tight.

When his act was over, Johnny came back into the dressing room furious and yelled at Mr. Snyder, "I don't want her in my act any more! She's not going to steal my show! Did you see her try to steal the show when she put that guitar strap over her shoulder so it would show off her tits?"

Mr. Snyder tried to calm him, but Johnny was serious. Stealing the show had been the farthest thing from my mind, although naturally I wanted to be accepted by the audience. But I hadn't done anything intentionally to detract from Johnny, and I told him so.

Finally, Johnny agreed to allow me to finish the remaining two shows that evening, and I was especially careful each time I placed the guitar strap over my shoulder not to make any unnecessary moves with my body. Mr. Snyder told me not to worry, that he would take care of Johnny, and he made arrangements to meet me the next day at a dress store located not too far from the Donut Shop after I got off work. I needed a costume change, he said.

I stayed awake most of the rest of that night after I had written a letter to my mother telling her all about my new adventure and my new job and my new name. I was in show business. I, Fannie Belle Fleming, was in show business. I was Blaze Starr!

6

The following day I met Red Snyder at a specialty shop on Connecticut Avenue. Never in my life had I seen so many beautiful dresses. I tried on several at Mr. Snyder's suggestion, and each time he stood back a distance and had me turn around so he could observe. The dress he finally chose was a low-cut black gown that clung snugly to my body. He then picked out a low-cut black brassiere to wear under the dress (my own white 38-D showed at the neck) and panties and accessories, including long, red gloves and high-heeled shoes.

As we left the shop and walked towards his car, I asked why he had chosen such a fancy outfit. I loved it, but it didn't seem right for picking a guitar, I said. He glanced at me from the corner of his eye and said, "You are going to strip tonight."

"I am going to strip? Are you crazy? What are you talking about?" I asked, horrified at the mere suggestion.

"Take it easy, now. Just take it easy and let me explain," he said, as he opened the car door for me.

I stood there on the sidewalk staring at him. He began to explain. "Well, I'll have to tell you. It's like this, Blaze. I had real trouble with Johnny last night because of you, and he threatened to quit. Now I know it doesn't mean anything to you, but I can't afford for him to walk away, and if you want to make it in show business, you are going to have to strip tonight, just like the other two girls I've got out there."

I sank down into the front car seat. The idea of taking my clothes off in public was totally shocking. I thought of my friends back in West Virginia. What would they think? What would Aunt Sally say? And Harriet? And how could I possibly explain such a thing to my mother? I decided that I could not do it and got out of Mr. Snyder's car again before he could close the door.

Mr. Snyder was irritated. "What in the hell do you want me to do, girl? Here I have given you a chance to get into show business, just spent eighty-seven dollars fitting you out, and you carry on like this. Now get back in the car, and let's talk this matter over without a scene."

I obeyed and got back into the car. It was true, he had been generous. As he drove down Connecticut Avenue, he sat silently, waiting for me to say something. Finally he looked at me and grinned. "You'll knock them dead with a body like you've got. You just wait and see," he said.

"But, Mr. Snyder, I ain't been raised to do a thing like this. My folks are all very religious, and they could never accept me doing a thing like this."

"You don't understand, Blaze. There isn't anything wrong with stripping. It's part of show business. It's an act just like any other dancing. You ever heard of a woman named Gypsy Rose Lee? She's a stripper, and believe me, she is big time. Now you just write home and tell your mom that you are a dancer. That's all you have to tell her. And by the way, how about you just calling me Red, and drop that Mr. business," he said, glancing towards me for a reaction.

I liked it when he called me Blaze. It had a certain show business glamour to it, and I kept saying it over and over in my mind as he talked. "But, Red, I have never danced. I would have no idea what to do," I argued.

"There's nothing to it. Just watch the other two girls and do what they do. Just bump and grind a little, that's all. In fact, why don't we drop by my apartment, and you can practice once," he suggested casually.

"In front of you?" I asked.

"Sure, why not? If I am going to be your manager, don't you think I ought to be your trainer, too?"

"Oh, no, I couldn't do that, no sir. Maybe tonight at the club, but not in your apartment with just you there."

"Okay, okay," he said. "It was just a suggestion; forget it."

"Well, I didn't mean it that way. I just don't think I should go to your place to practice. I don't mind you being my manager."

"You still haven't told me what you are going to do. I am ready to give you fifty dollars for the weekend, like I promised. That's a helluva lot more than you can make at the Donut Shop. You do want to be in show business, don't you?"

"Sure, but I've got to think about it. How about dropping me off at my place, and I'll call you and let you know definitely in an hour."

"Okay, that's fair enough."

"But, Red, there's something I think I should tell you first."

"Yeah, what's that?" he asked anxiously.

"I am only sixteen years old."

"My God, girl, I don't believe you. You look like you are eighteen or twenty. Are you telling me the truth?" he demanded.

"Yes, sir," I said slowly, feeling guilty.

"Well, that's it, then. I sure ain't going to get my ass in trouble over a sixteen-year-old runaway," he said sternly.

I began to cry, and I took a handkerchief from my handbag to wipe my eyes. "I'm sorry, Mr. Snyder, I should have said so earlier."

"Red, dammit, call me Red! How many times do I have to tell you?" he demanded.

He remained silent for the next few minutes as he sped towards my rooming house. Stopping the car in front, he looked over at me and asked, "How many people here in D.C. know you are only sixteen?" His voice had calmed considerably.

"You are the only one, Mr.—I mean Red. I haven't told another soul, so help me God."

"Do you think you can keep it to yourself?" he asked.

"Yes, sir, I promise with all my heart. I won't tell a living soul 'cause I don't want to go back to West Virginia. And, Red, if you'll not tell, I'll dance for you tonight, okay?"

He grinned all over his face. "You've got a deal, Blaze," he said and extended his hand.

I shook his hand and told him to pick me up at seven o'clock.

As I made my way to the dressing room that evening, my heart was pounding loudly, and I could feel a slight trembling of my legs. Red had told me that I could appear after the other two strippers, and that would give me a chance to observe them so that I could imitate their steps.

There was a strong smell of makeup in the dressing

room. A small dressing table was covered with tubes of lipstick, rouge, and assorted types of powder, and a full-length mirror was fastened to the wall next to it. Just as I hung my new black gown on a clothes rack, a woman came rushing in and introduced herself as Tiny Lou. She handed me two pasties and a bikini bottom. It was the first pair of pasties I had ever seen, and the rear of the bikini bottom was made of see-through lace. My hands trembled as I reached out for them.

"What the hell you shaking about, kid? If I had a set of tits like you, I would be in Hollywood."

"But I've never done anything like this before. I don't even know how to put these on."

"Well, take your damn clothes off, and I'll show you," she said as she sat down at the dressing table.

I was terribly embarrassed but was afraid not to follow Tiny's instructions. I carefully took off my street clothes and placed them on a chair, and turned to face Tiny.

"All I can say, kid, is that you've got one helluva set of boobs, and if you use them right they are going to take you a helluva way," she muttered as she fastened the two pasties securely to the nipples of my breasts. "Okay, you can take it from there, and for God's sake quit shaking. There ain't nothing to it. All you've got to do is get out there and shake your tits and wiggle your ass, and everything else will take care of itself." She winked at me as she left the room.

She made it sound so cheap, she frightened me all the more. I had never heard a woman talk in such vulgar terms. I refused to look at myself in the mirror for fear that I would not go through with it. After Tiny left, I finished dressing. The pasties felt terribly sensitive under the black brassiere. The last thing I did was to put on the high heels, the first pair I had ever worn. They made me feel awkward, and I feared I would fall for certain if I tried to dance in them. I walked back and forth, back and forth across the small room to get the feel.

I could vaguely hear Johnny Wise singing and occasional applause from the audience. The strippers would follow his act. There was a knock on the door, and Red entered before I had a chance to open it.

"My, just look at you! Aren't you a doll," he said, clasping his arms around me. "Say, Blaze, there's going to be a big party tonight after your act at a friend's house, and you are invited. There's going to be a lot of important show business people there, and it will be a good opportunity for you to meet them."

I smiled and pulled his arms away in a manner not to embarrass him and began putting on the long red gloves he had bought me.

"Okay, Tiny Lou is getting ready to begin her act so get out there and watch her. There's nothing to it; just dance back and forth across the stage," he said.

I made my way to a side entrance off the stage just as the five-piece band began to play. Tiny stepped past me onto the stage, dancing slowly back and forth. A spotlight followed every step. After three or four minutes, she casually slipped out of her gown, and there were whistles from the audience. She continued to move around the stage, constantly smiling, and finally reaching up and unfastening her brassiere and tossing it to one of the men who were sitting up close. The audience roared, and the man who caught the top stood up and held it high in the air for everyone to see. Tiny threw him a kiss, as she continued to move gracefully to the rhythm of the music.

It all looked simple enough as far as the dancing was concerned. The problem was having to undress in public. Rather than watch the other stripper, I went back to the dressing room and attempted to imitate Tiny's dancing step. By that time I was really scared stiff, and the longer

I waited, the more the tension mounted. Just before the second stripper finished, I went back to the stage door and watched her complete her act.

I thought I would be next, but the master of ceremonies introduced a young comedian, and Red told me to go back to the dressing room to wait, that it would probably be another ten minutes before I would go on stage.

Waiting for the comedian to finish was an eternity, but finally Red came and said it was time. I stood at the stage entrance until there was a roll of the drums and the master of ceremonies said, "Ladies and gentlemen, I would like to introduce—for the first time on stage as a stripper—Miss Blaze Starr!"

There was loud applause from the audience and then the sound of the band. I took a deep breath and stepped on stage. I could barely see the faces of the men sitting alongside the stage staring upward. I began trying to match some kind of motion to the music, scarcely hearing it in my daze, still frightened beyond description. After a minute or so, I realized that I was moving too fast. About the same time, I saw Red signal with his hand for me to slow down.

Four or five minutes passed, and I had made no effort to remove my gown. Red was now making motions for me to slip out of it, and someone in the audience shouted, "Take it off; take it off!"

By this time I had kicked off the high heels and was dancing barefoot. Standing almost motionless with my eyes closed tight, I unfastened my gown and let it fall to the floor. There were loud yells and whistles from the audience. Finally, I opened my eyes and began moving again, back and forth across the stage.

Red was now motioning for me to take off the top. Even in my half-conscious state, it struck me that he appeared more eager than the audience. I danced to the opposite end of the stage and, with my back to the audience, unfastened my brassiere and threw it over my shoulder just as Tiny had done. Then I turned to face the audience with my bosom exposed. I was through the hard part. Again there were whistles, yells, and loud applause. Red was also clapping his hands.

As I left the stage and ran to my dressing room, I could still hear the audience yelling and applauding. It was a good feeling. I knew they had liked me.

Red came rushing into the dressing room behind me, and I grabbed a towel and draped it over my shoulders to hide my bosom. "Hey, baby, you were great, just absolutely great! I told you it was not that difficult," he said excitely.

I smiled and suggested that he had better leave so that I could dress. As he went out the door, he reminded me about the party and said we would be leaving as soon as I was ready.

I sat on my dressing bench several minutes thinking about what I had just done, thinking mostly about my mother and father and how they would accept me as a stripper. I wanted to tell them, I wanted them to know that I was in show business. I just knew they would be proud of me. I decided that I would write a letter as soon as I got home that night and explain everything.

Thirty minutes later, I was with Red traveling towards Arlington, Virginia, to the party. He was jovial and in good spirits. "Yes, sir, tomorrow I am going to have my attorney prepare a contract for you to sign. I am going to be your agent, and you are going to travel all around the United States. I am going to make you a star."

Everything was happening so quickly I could hardly think straight. The idea of being a star was so unbelievable I could not even respond to his statement.

"That's what you want to be, isn't it? A big star! That calls for a drink. Reach in the glove compartment and get my bottle, and let's have a drink to that. What do you say?''

Without answering, I opened the glove compartment, took the cap off the bottle, and handed it to him.

''No, no, you take a drink first,'' he insisted.

To oblige him I took a small taste and reached the bottle to him. He turned it up and, before taking a big drink, said, ''Here's to the new star, Blaze Starr!''

We pulled into a driveway, and I could see in the shadows a large, elaborate house. He parked at the front entrance, and we went inside. To my amazement there seemed to be no one around.

''Where is everyone else?'' I asked him. ''I thought you said there was going to be a lot of important people here.''

He looked at me and grinned, then took a key from his pocket, and locked the front door. ''There's you and me.''

''What's going on here?'' I demanded.

''Come and and sit down. You and I have got to have a talk if we are going to be business partners,'' he said as he turned the bottle he was carrying to his lips and had another big drink.

''But when are all the people coming?'' I insisted.

''There ain't no more people. I told you, Blaze, just you and me, goddammit. And like I say, we've got a lot of things to talk about.''

Even in my anxiety, I could not help but notice the lavishness of the house and the furniture as we walked into the living room. I sat down on the edge of a sofa, apprehensively. Red walked over and sat down beside me and placed his bottle on a table in front of the sofa. I slid away to the other end.

''Now look, I didn't come here to play games with you, little lady. If we are going to be business partners, then we've got to be partners all the way, do you understand?'' He had moved to the end of the sofa where I was sitting and commenced lallygagging all over me. I squirmed and tried to break away, but he grabbed me and held me firmly against the sofa.

"Goddammit, calm down, girl. I ain't going to hurt you," he said as he shook me lightly. Then his voice calmed. "Blaze, I think you are the prettiest girl I have ever seen." He released his grip and was now just sitting there playing with my ear. I was frozen with fear, and every muscle in my body tensed. He once again began slobbering all over my neck, feeling my breast with one hand and trying to pull my dress up with the other.

I wondered what kind of mess I had got myself into now. If this awful man gets hold of me, I thought, no other man in the whole world will ever have me, I was really disgusted as well as thoroughly frightened by this time. I knew there was no escape through the front door because he had the key in his pocket. And I knew I had no possibility of resisting him for long. He was a hulking man who could easily harm me seriously.

Hoping to buy some time, I struggled to pull away, saying, "Okay, take it easy. If it's got to be this way, at least I would like to take a shower."

He calmed down and released me from his grip. "I guess that's good enough," he said. He walked to another room and came back and handed me a black see-through negligee. "Here, put this on after you have your bath."

I had kicked off my new high-heeled shoes again because they pinched my feet. Red picked them up, took my handbag and his bottle, and then followed me halfway up the stairs. I was greatly relieved when he suddenly sat down heavily on the steps with his bottle. But when I asked for my handbag, he refused to give it to me. I was afraid to press him or to ask for my shoes.

In total panic, I went up the rest of the stairs and inside the bathroom, shut the door, and locked it. The bathroom had a small window, and I immediately, thankfully, thought of crawling through it. I knew I had only a few minutes. I turned the water on in the shower, then opened the window to see if I could get through it, and what was outside. Fortunately it was only a short drop to a lower roof from which I thought I could jump safely to the ground. After a short struggle, I managed to squeeze the upper part of my body through and knew I could make it the rest of the way.

"What's taking you so long? Hurry up!" I heard Red shout. His voice was mean and ugly.

It was just like Blair Mountain all over again. I felt sick. But this time my anxiety turned to anger, and I pushed myself back into the bathroom, determined to take some kind of action. In a voice deliberately soft, I called out, "I'll be right down, honey. Just another minute or two."

I crammed a washcloth into the overflow drain of the bathtub and turned the water on full force, then hurriedly wiggled out the window, barefooted and without my handbag. The jump from the roof was probably ten feet or more, but I didn't hesitate. Luckily, I was not injured. I ran towards the street and on several blocks through the darkness of Arlington before I was able to hail a taxi. I explained to the cab driver that I had run into a problem and had to leave barefooted and without my handbag. I promised I would give him my watch if he would drive me home. He seemed dubious, but by now I was bawling, and he finally agreed. Soon we were crossing the bridge over the Potomac, and before much longer I was safe in the security of my small room. My tears had dried. I went straight to sleep, exhausted.

The next day Red Snyder stormed into the Donut Shop ranting and raving. "You have cost me thousands of dollars in damage to my friend's house. The water has ruined everything! I didn't know what you were up to until it trickled down the stairs under me, and then I was another ten or fifteen minutes breaking the door down. And when

I did, the water gushed all the way into the living room." His voice was growing louder and more aggrieved. "How could you have done that to me?"

Angry myself, but fearful that he was going to become violent, I rushed to my boss in the back room. "This stranger is yelling at me, and I don't even know him," I said.

Red continued to holler until the manager threatened to call the police if he didn't leave. As he went out the door, he turned and yelled back at me, "I'll get even with you!"

I was out of show business as fast as I had got into it.

7

Serving donuts had been fun at the start. A lot of people came into the small, busy shop, and there was always plenty of kidding and a nice, brisk pace. But now it seemed to have lost its charm. I found myself daydreaming half the time about show business—about being a big star, with folks wanting my autograph, and newspapermen interviewing me and taking my picture. Even though I had been scared nearly stiff during my one and only appearance as a stripper, all I had to do was close my eyes for a second there behind the counter stacked with donuts, and I could hear the yells of approval, the whistles, the applause.

I thought of my cousin Molly O'Day, a big country singer who was very popular back in West Virginia. My mother and father often talked about her success, and we always listened to her radio program every Saturday night from station WWVA in Wheeling on a secondhand battery radio my father had managed to buy a year before I left home. It was sometimes a contrary contraption and all the more complicated because of its antenna wire, which was stretched about three hundred feet from the corner of our house to the corn crib, and another wire running out the back window and down to serve as a ground wire. When the sound faded out, which was often the case, my dad would pour salt water on the ground wire to make it come in stronger. When the adults weren't around and the sound faded, one of us kids would just pee on the ground wire. It had the same effect.

I used to walk five miles to a relative's house on Twelve Pole Creek quite often to listen to some of Molly's records on what we called their talking machine. Everyone bragged about how much money she was making and what a big star she had become. And I used to slip off to the corn crib and sing at the top of my voice and pick the guitar, all the time pretending I was Molly O'Day. I don't know whether I sounded much like her, but it was sure fun.

Of course there was a difference between singing country and gospel music and taking your clothes off in front of a bunch of men. And every time I daydreamed about being a stripper, my fantasy would be interrupted by thoughts of my mother and father and what they would think if they knew I had actually stripped at the Quonset Hut. How could I explain it to them? I remembered their talking about the indecency of some woman on the creek who wore her dresses slightly above her knees. Red Snyder had dignified stripping by calling it an art, but it seemed kind of unlikely that I could persuade my parents to accept this viewpoint. Still I went out and bought myself a pair of high heels, and in the privacy of my little room, I practiced bumps and grinds night after night. I knew I wanted to become a star, and stripping looked like my best opportunity.

At least the Donut Shop was an excellent place to meet people. Sooner or later I figured a "good" Red Snyder would come in and rediscover me. But though that hope sustained me as I worked by day and practiced routines by night and waited, nothing seemed to happen. Finally, I concluded that if I were ever to have another opportunity to get into show business, I would have to do something on my own.

One of the boarders had left a magazine with a picture of a stripper on the cover lying on the kitchen table of the rooming house. I sneaked it under my coat and took it to my room where I read it from cover to cover. One story talked about all the strip clubs in Baltimore and how popular stripping had become. I had read about Baltimore when I was in the eight grade, but I had no idea it was so close to Washington, D.C., until the next day when one of the girls at the Donut Shop told me it was only forty or fifty miles away.

I read that magazine about every night for two weeks and decided that if I was ever to get a chance to become a stripper, Baltimore would be the place to go. I thought about moving, but I hadn't been able to save enough money, so I continued to work at the Donut Shop. I thought a lot about all the strip clubs in Baltimore and was just dying to get a chance to go to one of them. But I couldn't get up enough nerve to go alone, and no boy in his right mind would ever take a girl to a strip place, I knew. It seemed hopeless. If it was so difficult for me even to visit a strip club, it would be nearly impossible ever to get to dance in one of them, I thought. Still I was slowly becoming determined that if I did manage some day to get my foot through the front door of a strip place, I was going to ask the boss for a job if it burst every gut in me.

Several months passed. I was on my second date with Jim Bower, a young government worker, and he took me to Baltimore to a movie. After the show, he asked me what I wanted to do, and, with my voice choking, I asked him if he had ever visited any of the strip clubs. I rushed through the suggestion that I would like to go so fast he hardly understood me, and I had to repeat myself.

"A strip place?" he said, sounding astonished.

"Yeah. I'm a stripper."

"You're a stripper? What about the Donut Shop, Belle?" He looked shocked and disbelieving.

I told him my stage name was Blaze Starr and that I was holding down two jobs because needed the extra money to send home. "But keep it a secret, Jim, please. I'm afraid I'll lose my job at the Donut Shop if they find out."

He was a nice young man and obviously bewildered by my revelation—true in spirit if somewhat exaggerated. But he agreed to take me. I grabbed his hand enthusiastically, and we ran the two blocks to his car. Within minutes, we were in East Baltimore.

As we approached what was called "The Block," I hit Jim on the leg and yelled, "Oh God, look at it! It's all lit up just like they said in the magazine."

"Watch it, you'll cause a wreck," Jim said as he slowed the car to find a parking spot.

"Look at the lights! Just look at that, would you! Oh, there's the Two O'Clock Club. They had a picture of it in the magazine. It used to be a restaurant, and some president of the United States ate there once. That's where I want to go."

"What's this magazine bit you are talking about?" Jim inquired as he stopped the car and began to crowd into a parking slot.

"Oh, nothing. Just a magazine I read a few weeks back about this place. Would you look at those neon lights!"

I jumped out of the car before Jim could get around to open the door for me. As we walked back towards the Two O'Clock Club, we stopped in front of two or three other strip clubs and looked at the pictures of the strippers on display at the door. We could hear the drums roll and the horns blare all the way out on the street.

In front of one of the clubs a little man dressed in a fancy tuxedo was yelling at the top of his voice, "Step right in, ladies and gentlemen, step right in. See the most ravishing beauties in the world performing live on stage."

As we slowly walked past, trying to peep inside, he took a step or two towards us and said, "It's all here—nowhere else. Step right in. No waiting. See the ravishing beauties." I held on to Jim's arm, and we walked on past.

My heart was pounding almost as furiously as it had the night I stripped at the Quonset Hut when we entered the doorway of the Two O'Clock Club. The place was crowded, and we had to wait in line for almost thirty minutes before we were seated. From the entrance I could see that the stage at the club extended almost the full length of the room. It was encircled by bar stools that put the customers—they were all men—on eye level with the performers.

We were seated at a table on a small landing overlooking the stage. It was an excellent vantage point for observing the strippers. A small band played as one girl after another danced back and forth down the length of the stage. They looked so graceful. Jim held my hand on the table, but his eyes were on the stage.

I sat there debating whether I should ask for the boss. Back in my room I had had everything planned. I knew exactly what I was going to say. But now that it was real, everything was different. I almost wished I were back in my room. It was all so easy there. I kept telling myself that if I didn't do it now, I would regret it later. You will wake up tomorrow and regret every minute of the evening if you don't go ahead, I told myself. Finally, I took a deep breath and asked a waitress if I could see the boss. I told her I would like to talk to him about a job as a stripper and gave her the name Blaze Starr, which she wrote down on a pad. Jim seemed puzzled and amazed, but he didn't say anything.

The waitress came back a few minutes later and told me that I had caught the boss in a good mood and that he would be out to talk with me in a few minutes. I fought desperately to maintain my composure. Much as I wanted to appear calm, my hands were trembling as I waited for him. I tried talking with Jim, but by this time he was preoccupied with one of the strippers who had sat down at a table next to ours.

It seemed an hour before Mr. Goodman, the owner of the Two O'Clock Club, came up and introduced himself. He asked Jim very politely if he'd mind if I went with him to his office for a few minutes and then led me though the audience to a tiny office located behind the band. He sat down at a small desk, and I remained standing.

"So you are a stripper," he said as he thumbed through some papers on his desk. "Is that all you?"

"What do you mean?" I asked nervously.

"Your bosom. You know in this business that's very important. I just want to make sure you don't have falsies on."

"Well, I'll show you," I said and reached to unbutton my blouse.

"No, no," he interrupted. "If you say it's you, it's you. Where are you from?"

"West Virginia."

He grinned. "They don't wear shoes down there, do they?"

"Well, most folks do, except they are not too good with high heels."

He asked my age, and when I told him eighteen, he looked at me carefully and said, "They come and go here. Babies come and go, and old ladies come and go. But if you are sixteen, you're lucky."

Tears came to my eyes, for I felt certain he would not

hire me now. I stood there waiting for him to tell me to leave.

Instead, he asked, "Why do you want to become a stripper?"

I explained to him that I had stripped at the Quonset Hut and told him how thrilling that had been and how I'd been practicing in my room in Washington every night since. I also explained about the incident with Red Snyder.

He roared with laughter. "Well, I can't let you work downstairs because of your age, but I have a theater upstairs where you only have to be fourteen since we don't sell drinks up there. The only law we have to worry about upstairs is the child labor law. I'd be willing to give you a chance there."

"Thank you, Mr. Goodman, thank you," I said. "I will work hard, and you will be proud of me, I promise." I was so excited that I could hardly talk.

He had me wait until he brought his wife back to the office so that I could meet her. Mrs. Goodman served as club hostess during the weekends and also ran the theater. She was as friendly as her husband, and I thought how nice it was going to be working for them instead of a Red Snyder. Jim did not believe me when I told him what had happened. He was quiet and seemed kind of embarrassed as we drove back to D.C. I was so keyed up I sang along with the radio all the way.

The next day I paid my room rent, called the Donut Shop to tell the manager I wouldn't be in any more, and caught a bus to Baltimore with all my belongings. That same evening, I went to work for Mr. and Mrs. Goodman. I was introduced to all the girls, and Big Lulu, a tall, husky peroxide blonde in her early thirties, offered to put me up for the night until I could find myself a room. There was one other young girl who worked in the theater, but the rest appeared to be in their late twenties.

The theater was about half full when I did my first performance. Although I was terribly nervous before I went on stage, it was nothing like my experience at the Quonset Hut. The many nights of practice in my room paid off, and once I was moving to the music, I felt all right. I wore a green satin gown that Mr. Goodman loaned me from the theater wardrobe, with a transparent net over my bosom and a bikini bottom.

There was a marked difference between the audience at the Two O'Clock Club and the one at the Quonset Hut. At the Two O'Clock Club, the audience was more subdued, and I was beginning to wonder whether I was pleasing them. There was applause as I let my gown drop to the floor but no loud whistles. I continued to bump and grind across the stage, forcing a smile as I unfastened my brassiere, leaving only the transparent net. This time the applause was louder and continued until I completed my performance and the curtains closed.

I felt pleased as I walked off the stage with my gown gathered under my arm. Mr. Goodman had been watching from the side of the stage and nodded his approval as I went into my small dressing room.

It was almost 3 A.M. when Big Lulu and I climbed the flight of steps to her two-room apartment. I was terribly tired but still wide awake because of all the excitement.

"It ain't much," Big Lulu said as she unlocked the door. "But I ain't here much either, so I guess it's good enough."

There was a musty smell in the apartment, and she cracked the window a little to allow for some fresh air. I slouched down on a couch, and Big Lulu turned on the radio and lit herself a cigar. I thought it was a little funny for a woman to be smoking a cigar. June and I used to slip out behind the corn crib and smoke corn silks in a corncob pipe, but we never thought once about a woman smoking a cigar.

"Want a cigar, baby?"

"Oh, no I don't smoke."

She walked over and sat down next to me on the couch. "Let me fix you a sandwich," she said.

"Golly, I sure could go for that. I just remembered I haven't had a thing to eat today since breakfast."

I raised up to help, but Big Lulu pushed me back and said, "You just sit there and rest. I'll fix it."

We sat there and ate baloney sandwiches and talked until finally she suggested we go to bed.

"I suppose I am to sleep on the couch?"

"No, we share my bed. It's big enough for both."

"Okay." I opened my suitcase and pulled out a pair of pajamas. Big Lulu stripped bare and jumped into bed. Being last to get into bed, I flipped off the light switch and crawled in beside her.

A window shade was half open, and a street light partially lit the room. Occasionally, I could hear a car pass. It was difficult for me to go to sleep. My mind was all blurry and my thoughts all mixed up. The fatigue and excitement had gotten to me.

Big Lulu was also tossing and turning. She moved over against me, almost crowding me out. I didn't know for sure whether she was completely asleep. I didn't want to take a chance on disturbing her by moving. A few minutes passed, and she put her arm over my waist. It was uncomfortable, but again I was afraid of disturbing her so I just sort of lay there in misery. Suddenly her hand moved under my pajama top and began caressing my breast. My first thought was, "Boy, what a dream she's having." But suddenly I realized that she was not asleep. She was breathing heavily. I jumped from the bed.

"What's the matter, honey?" Big Lulu said softly.

"My God, what's coming off?" I asked. "I'm getting out of here!"

"Don't, please," she begged. "Come on to bed with me. Please. Don't leave now."

I turned the light on and began dressing. I was terrified. Never in my life had I ever heard of a woman carrying on like that with another woman.

She was sobbing as I hurriedly dressed. "Please don't leave me. Please don't. I love you. I love you."

"Oh my God, let me out of here," I thought to myself. I grabbed my suitcase and ran towards the door.

Big Lulu started cursing and calling me all sorts of names. "Get out of here, then, you bitch! Get out of here!" she yelled. She screamed hysterically and rolled over and buried her head in her pillow as I fled from the room.

I ran six or eight blocks and was ready to collapse when I finally was able to catch a taxi.

"Where to, lady?"

"Take me to the nearest hotel."

"Sure. There's one just three blocks from here. Sure is a nice night, isn't it?"

"Yeah. It really is." My voice sounded kind of shaky to me. "If he only knew what I've been through," I thought to myself.

I managed to get a room for $2.50. It was nearly 5:30 and beginning to turn light before I got to bed.

I didn't say anything to anyone about Big Lulu, but she would not speak to me the next evening. I don't know if it was my imagination, but all of the girls seemed kind of stand-offish, and my efforts to strike up a conversation were ignored. They never did get what you'd call friendly, any of them, and one or two really hassled me from the start.

I hardly had time to worry about the attitude of the girls, though, for I was busy making myself another gown. The green satin from the wardrobe was nice, but I wanted something really special of my own. I bought gold satin from Baltimore's leading department store and red and green feathers from a costume shop to trim it with. Since I didn't have a sewing machine, I had to do all the stitching by hand, and I worked on the gown during the breaks between my five daily performances. Once or twice when I was stitching, I heard Grandma Fannie's voice saying, "Don't pull the thread too tight, Fannie Belle," and it scared me to think what she would say if she knew I was using her teaching to make me a dress to take off in public. But it was a beautiful gown when I finished, and it won me many compliments.

After about six months, Mr. Goodman told me that his business had doubled since I had been performing and that I deserved the credit, so he was putting my name and picture outside. This really infuriated some of the girls who had been there longer than I had, and the conflict that had existed between them and me from the very beginning flared up. Once day when I came to work, I found my gold gown cut into a hundred pieces and taped to the wall of my dressing room. Heartbroken and in tears, I ran to Mr. Goodman, who tried to cheer me up by replacing the gown with one of the best he had from downstairs. He and Mrs. Goodman both gave the girls a stern warning to leave me alone, but it only made matters worse.

The next night when I went to my dressing room, Big Lulu and two other girls grabbed me. "Hold the little bitch," Big Lulu yelled. "I'll teach her to squeal to Goodman the next time."

I struggled to free myself, but one of the girls had managed to twist my arm behind my back, and every time I made a move, she twisted harder until the pain was unbearable.

"Get those scissors over there. Let's cut her goddamn hair off."

"No, no, please," I begged.

"Shut up, bitch, it's too damn late for you to beg now.

We ain't got room for you around here. If we can't get rid of you one way, we'll do it another," Big Lulu shouted.

The two girls held me while Big Lulu hacked at my hair. Then they threw me on the floor and ran giggling from the dressing room. I guess I must have lain there on the floor for an hour crying my heart out, and I was hysterical when Mr. Goodman came into my dressing room to find out why I wasn't ready to go on stage and demanding to know what had happened.

Between sobs I explained what the girls had done. Mr. Goodman, infuriated, rushed from the room and had the three girls out of the building before they could even gather their belongings. Then he and Mrs. Goodman came back to the dressing room to console me and summoned a hair stylist who was able to shape up what hair I had left so it didn't look too bad.

As time passed, I became more determined to move downstairs and dance in the club proper. Mr. Goodman was bringing in a star stripper every two weeks, and I always went downstairs between my acts to watch them work in hopes of improving my own dancing. I also bought every book and magazine I could find about famous strippers such as Gypsy Rose Lee, Ann Corio, Margie Hart, and Henda Wassa.

My continued begging finally persuaded Mr. Goodman to give me a chance in the club. At least I was getting closer to being eighteen. In addition to my five acts upstairs, he agreed to let me perform twice a night downstairs. I was overjoyed with the opportunity and determined to be successful. It turned out to be a strenuous pace, but I loved it.

I had been working only three weeks downstairs when a new stripper who danced to a drum solo and was different from any other stripper I had ever seen was featured at the club. I still remember watching her dance. It was an unforgettable experience. If only I could be like her, I thought, I would have it made.

The next night when it came my turn to perform, I asked the band to play a drum solo. They agreed, and I mimicked the featured stripper's bump-and-grind technique. Her husband was enthusiastic about my act and wanted to hire me immediately to travel with them. She, however, was furious with me and told Mr. Goodman that she would under no circumstances continue to dance at the club if he was going to allow some "wild-eyed kid" to steal her act. At Mr. Goodman's request, I apologized to her and promised I would not copy her act again.

The following week another star, one of the most beautiful strippers I have ever seen, was featured. She had long black hair and a perfect build to go with it. She wore a black velvet gown, white beret, and very high-heeled shoes that had a big ball of white fur on the toes. She held a long cigarette holder between her fingers and carried a small evening bag. It was a stunning outfit. The club was packed each night she performed, and the men gaped and drooled when she stripped.

I could not resist the temptation of making an outfit like hers. The very next morning I went out and bought enough black velvet for the gown and substituted white maribou for the white ermine on her dress. That same afternoon, I duplicated her costume. What I didn't have time to sew, I glued, and that night I went on stage ahead of her, not only wearing a gown like hers, but copying her act as well.

At first she thought I had stolen her costume and went immediately to tell Mr. Goodman so. He tried to calm her and told her that he was sure I hadn't stolen the outfit; he guessed I had copied it and that I was just a kid from the sticks who didn't know any better. She was not soothed. When I danced off stage and returned to my dressing room, she was waiting there brandishing a big butcher knife she had picked up from the bar where it was used to slice oranges and lemons. She chased me all over the club yelling and screaming at the top of her voice before Mr. Goodman and the bartender finally subdued her and wrested the knife from her hand.

By the next day, she had calmed down, and before she left at the end of the week, this generous woman give me a friendly lecture. "You've got a lot to learn," she said. "You've got to learn professional courtesy. You just can't go stealing everybody's act. You must realize that we work hard to originate and develop our own individual performances, and it is very irritating, to say the least, to see some other little two-bit new stripper trying to imitate you. Especially if the two of you happen to be performing on the same stage!"

It was the first time anyone had really made me aware of what I was doing, and I felt quite ashamed of myself. Mr. Goodman also gave me a kind reprimand. "Blaze," he said, "you can't continue to disrupt this club like you have been doing. It'll be so that I can't get any girls."

I apologized and told him that one of these days I was going to be a big star and that he would be proud of me.

Naturally I didn't wear any copied outfits after that. Instead, I made myself a new costume of my own inspiration. The skirt was black and cut off well above the knees with slits up each side. The top was a red sequined jacket, fastened only at the waist. It was accented with a black sequined beret. I looked pretty "whore-ified," but that was the whole idea. The band would play "Boulevard of Broken Dreams," then go into a drum solo abut halfway through my act as I strutted back and forth, shaking and twisting every part of my body in all sorts of titillative movements. The men loved it. I no longer had to copy other strippers. I was as good as anybody, and the audience let me know it.

Dancing downstairs was much more exciting than in the upstairs theater. Upstairs the dancers did not have an opportunity to meet the audience, whereas downstairs they could socialize with the customers between acts. The money was much better, too. Besides a salary of $105 a week, a girl could expect to receive $50 to $75 in tips. Men were always giving me money, some of which I used to buy gowns and high-heeled shoes, my "work clothes." The remainder I would send home to my mother.

I had written my mother about Red Snyder and about my brief encounter with show business while I was still in Washington, but I had not told her that I had stripped at the Quonset Hut. When I went to work at the Two O'Clock Club, however, I decided I had to break the news to her.

I wrote and explained that I was a burlesque dancer. Obviously, it didn't occur to her what I was really doing—dancing up and down the stage, teasing men, and taking my clothes off—for she immediately wrote back and told me how happy she was for me. But when she began to tell the neighbors that I was a burlesque dancer, they apparently thought I was just a whore up in Baltimore selling it. This reaction from the folks on Twelve Pole Creek hurt deeply, and I was concerned for the position I had put my mother and father in. I wanted very much for my parents and family to be proud, to be able to say that their daughter was in show business just like Molly O'Day.

A few weeks later, I wrote my mother again and told her that I was no longer a burlesque dancer but was an exotic dancer. Shortly after starting to work at the theater, I had made myself a belly-dancing outfit with some gauze scarves and bought a pair of toe shoes. I figured if a person was really going to learn to be a dancer, she ought to learn to dance in toe shoes. I had a picture made in the outfit, posing as a ballet dancer, pretty well draped in the scarves, and sent it to my mother. Now when somebody asked her, "How's Fannie Belle?" she would show the picture and say, "She's working in Baltimore. She's an exotic dancer, and she's dancing in a show." This seemed like a more acceptable profession, and that picture put a stop to the neighborhood gossip for a while.

All went well until some other pictures of me, in pasties and a G-string, started appearing in girlie magazines. Someone back on Twelve Pole Creek managed to get hold of a couple of the magazines and showed them to my mother. She was understandably upset, and I had a lot of explaining to do. Finally, though, I convinced her that my exotic dancing was legitimate show business, and as the months passed, she became very proud of my accomplishments. I continued to send home a little money each time I wrote and frequently sent boxes of clothing to my younger brothers and sisters. Mom always wrote back and reminded me to remember how she had raised me, warning me not to go out with strangers.

8

The first time I saw Carroll Glorioso, I thought he was the handsomest man I had ever seen. He was the owner of the Club Diamond on the 600 block of East Baltimore, and all the girls at the Two O'Clock Club, where he was a frequent visitor, were after him. I had been working at the Two O'Clock Club almost two years when Mr. Goodman first introduced me to Carroll, and afterwards I was a constant companion at his table.

One thing led to another, and Carroll and I soon began seeing each other on a regular basis. Six months later, he asked me to marry him, and I said yes, but not until he agreed to allow me to continue with my stripping career. When I announced my plans to Mr. and Mrs. Goodman, they were very happy for me, and the following Tuesday Mr. Goodman closed the club for an evening and invited more than a hundred people to a party to celebrate the impending marriage.

Carroll and I were married in a simple ceremony in Baltimore and left the same day for a two-week honeymoon in Mexico. It was the happiest day of my life since I'd left Newground Hollow. We planned to live simply. He would continue to operate the Club Diamond, I would continue dancing at the Two O'Clock Club, and we would move into a new house on Coronado Road.

In the beginning, everything happened just as we had planned, and it was fun being a housewife. But the pleasant routines of our marriage were soon to be interrupted. That fall I received a tremendous break. *Esquire* magazine was doing a feature story on the city of Baltimore, and more or less by accident the young reporter who was assigned to the story visited the Two O'Clock Club and caught my performance. I spent the next three days in interviews with him and posing for photographs, and two months later Blaze Starr was featured in the pages of *Esquire*.

I could hardly believe it. I visited practically every newsstand in Baltimore and purchased more than fifty copies, and I sent fifteen of them to my mother to pass out to all my friends and relatives on Twelve Pole Creek. Everyone at the Two O'Clock Club, especially Mr. Goodman, was overwhelmed by my appearance in a national magazine.

Mr. Goodman called me into his office the day after the article appeared and, in a very somber but pleased voice, said, "Blaze, this is the biggest opportunity you have ever had. You have always wanted to be a star, and now we can book you in all the clubs all across the United States. We will feature you as the '*Esquire* girl,' and if you would like, I will be your manager."

I readily agreed with Mr. Goodman's suggestion, and he began making arrangements to book me in other clubs as the featured star. I could see the disappointment in Carroll's eyes when I told him I would be going on the road and appearing in other cities. But we needed the money, and he reluctantly consented. We planned to renovate the

Club Diamond with the extra money that I would be making.

During the next few weeks I bought myself some of the fanciest gowns I could find in the Baltimore and Washington area. I went to Garfinckel's, to Erlebacher's, Rizik's, Hutzler's—all the stylish stores. Some of the dresses, of course, I had to alter a little—a dart here, a zipper there. In the meantime, Mr. Goodman booked me in Philadelphia at a place called the Wedge. I replaced Julie Gibson, the club's star, who was on vacation. Within a week business doubled, and I was held over.

Sensing for the first time that publicity was a must if I was going to become a big star, I began thinking up ways to attract attention from the news media. While I was still at the Wedge, I decided to become "the panther girl." For $750 I bought a young male leopard, only two months old and as tame as a house cat. My idea was to teach him to take my clothes off. In order to accomplish this, I pinned small pieces of steak on my gloves, my bra, my panties, the décolletage of my gown. After hours and hours of training, I got so that I could easily slip out of my clothes as he pulled off the pieces of steak, making it look as if he were really undressing me.

He was a cute, affectionate cat, and I bought a small ball for him to play with. On the day before I was to do my premiere act, he swallowed the ball and choked to death. I was very disappointed and also grieved at the death of the leopard. However, I wanted to go on with a cat act so I immediately wrote to New York to place an order for a black Asiatic panther. I purchased it from the Lewis Rue Animal Company, which imported wild animals. It cost me $1,100.

The panther arrived in about a month. At the start it was a mean little devil, constantly clawing, growling, and screaming like the "woman-ick" that roamed the mountains down home. But within two weeks, I was able to take it from its cage, and it paced about freely in my room. In fact, it acted as if I were its mother and insisted on sleeping with me.

By now I was so busy traveling that I did not have time to teach the panther to remove my clothes. I decided I would simply put it in a cage, then after I stripped I would enter the cage. Of necessity, the cat became a constant companion and traveled with me everywhere I went. This was a difficult arrangement, but it was the only way I could find time to train it.

When I went home for occasional visits with Carroll, I always took the panther with me. When the neighbors saw it in its cage in the yard, they began filing complaints with the Baltimore police department. They feared that it would escape and injure one of their children. After that, I kept the cage inside the house, and all the neighbors thought that I had gotten rid of it.

On my second trip to Philadelphia, where I once again was to be the featured star at the Wedge for a week, I decided that it was time to unleash the panther girl act. The cat had grown up, and although it was quite tame with me, it was ferocious with other people. When I checked into my Philadelphia hotel, I had to bribe the bellhops to get them to carry the heavy cage to my room. Although the hotel regulations prohibited animals in the room, they reluctantly agreed, but only after a thorough examination of the cage's fastenings.

That afternoon, I went window-shopping. When I returned to my room on the seventh floor, the panther was missing. I was horrified. It was impossible for the cat to have jumped from the window. But the door to my room had been locked when I came back. The hotel employees claimed to know nothing about it. I had no alternative but to report what had happened to the police. They issued an all-points bulletin for the citizens of Philadelphia to be on the alert for a black panther that was missing from a local hotel and presumed to have escaped. The newspapers and the radio and television stations carried the incident in headlines and news flashes. The city was in an uproar.

That night when I performed at the Wedge the room was filled to overflowing, and people had to be turned away. Reports came in from all over the city from people saying that they had seen the cat. One man claimed that the panther had attacked his small child, and he threatened to file suit against me. The police were ready to arrest me, and I had to plead with them in order to keep from going to jail. Three days later the cat was discovered at an animal shop in Philadelphia. The owner of the shop claimed that the panther had wandered in off the street.

The newspapers called the whole thing a publicity hoax. It was not. In my opinion, the animal had been stolen from my room. But I have to admit the publicity was great. The Wedge was filled to capacity every night. Since the cat seemed a little edgy from the experience, I did not introduce it into my act after all, but I became known as the "panther girl" anyway. I insisted on receiving a raise of $150 per week after my contract was extended.

After my engagement at the Wedge, I went on to New York for a week and checked in with the panther at the Forest Hotel. This time I had made previous arrangements with the hotel management, and they had agreed to allow me to keep the panther in my room. When I returned to my room on the second day, I was confronted by the Manhattan police and the fire department. The panther had accidentally turned on the water in the shower where I had made its bed, and the hotel was flooding. The hotel manager was in a panic and was pacing back and forth in front of my room. He had had to cut the water off in the entire wing of the hotel, since no one would go in to turn off the shower, and patrons were complaining.

The panther, too, was quite panicky. In fact, I don't think it would have allowed anyone in the room even if there had been a volunteer brave enough. I could hear it snarling and pacing, but feeling that I knew the cat well enough to calm it, I eased the door open and walked in. Its black fur was soaked, its eyes a shinier green than I had ever seen them. I held out my hand and said, "Come on, baby." But, apparently because of all the commotion, the cat obviously did not recognize me. It lunged at me and clawed my left eye. I ran from the room, fearing that my eye had been completely put out. My face was a bloody mess.

The police finally called the company from which I had purchased the cat, and they sent an animal trainer over to subdue it. Fortunately, my eye was not seriously injured, and I was able to return to work after a week. However, I was afraid to get near the cat so I decided to sell it back to the Lewis Rue Animal Company for $550. Thus, my dreams of using a panther in my act ended.

Some months later, I returned to Philadelphia for an engagement at the Black Cat Club. This time, determined to capitalize somehow on my fame as the panther woman, I developed a new gimmick. At the conclusion of my stripping act, I would lie down on a red shag carpet and pretend to *be* a panther, screaming and crawling all over the carpet, mentally seducing the men in the audience. This probably attracted as much attention as the panther would have itself. Maybe more.

It also attracted the attention of Police Captain Frank Rizzo.

I was doing my last act of the evening when my cat calls and crawling were interrupted by whistle-blowing from Captain Rizzo and three or four other policemen who trailed behind him through the crowded club towards the stage. I was terrified. The band quit playing, and I lay motionless, watching this giant of a policeman walk towards me. He yelled to Manny Jenkins, the owner of the club, "Get that screaming woman off the stage! Get that carpet off the stage. That's downright, outrageously filthy, dirty, obscene, and rude! I will not tolerate this kind of corruption in Philadelphia!" He jumped onto the stage and grabbed me by my arm and pulled me up from the carpet. "You're under arrest, young woman."

I had been arrested earlier while performing at Steve Brodie's Club Philadelphia, but the charge of performing a lewd act was dropped the next day without much fanfare. Even so, this time just as before, I began to cry for fear the news would reach my mother and the people back on Twelve Pole Creek. It would ruin my family's name. "Why are you arresting me, officer?" I sobbed.

"You heard what I said, young lady. I am not going to tolerate this obscene filth in the city of Philadelphia as long as I have any authority here." His voice was gruff.

"But my act was not obscene and filthy. I have a bikini bottom on. If you arrest me, it will be the end of my career," I pleaded tearfully.

"I am not interested in your career," he growled. "I am interested in the morals of the people of the city of Philadelphia. Come on, I am taking you to jail. Get your clothes on." He showed no sympathy and shoved me towards the dressing room.

Upset and frightened, I hastily put on my street clothes. By the time I dressed, all the customers had cleared the club, and Manny Jenkins was pacing back and forth, furious with Rizzo. "That son of a bitch is going to close down every stripping club in Philadelphia. He's going to ruin us all. Don't cry, I'll get you out," he added reassuringly.

"One of the girls is going to have to put the make on him or find out his price," the bartender chimed in as I left the club with Rizzo roughly clutching my arm.

The captain led me to the police cruiser and threw me in the back seat with three other strippers whom he had arrested at other clubs. He rode up front with a patrolman. The other girls were giggling and carrying on as if nothing had happened. I was still sobbing and crying. Being arrested and sitting in that police car made me feel like I really was a criminal.

A wire mesh grille separated the rear of the car from the two policemen. Captain Rizzo stretched around and peered through the grill and said in a stern voice. "Cry. Go on and cry all you want. It's not going to bother me one bit. But you'd better get your eyes straightened up for court tomorrow because you know all the newspaper reporters are going to be around. You liked all that publicity when you had us chasing through the city after your black panther. You like publicity, so you're going to make the paper tomorrow. How about that?"

The tone of his voice infuriated me, and I yelled back, "I wish we didn't have that wire between us, Cisco Kid!"

"Watch what you call me," he grunted. "You're only making it rough on yourself."

"I'd like to come up there and show you what kind of a panther I am. I'd claw your eyes out!"

"Shut up!" he barked. "Don't you have any respect at all for a policeman?"

With that, the other girls shouted with laughter and chimed in to harass Rizzo. One of them said, "I think he looks more like the Lone Ranger than he does the Cisco Kid."

"Big deal," I complained. "What was I doing against the law? I was simply performing a perfectly legitimate act with a total bikini bathing suit bottom, pasties, and mesh bra on. I was completely covered. And you have the nerve to call my act obscene and haul me off to jail like a common criminal. What right have you got?"

"It was your actions on stage. You looked like you were having relations right there on stage in front of everyone," Rizzo said.

"Maybe if you had relations every now and then, you wouldn't be so cranky," I snapped. "You must really hate your wife and be miserable at home to be so miserable to everybody else." By now I had become so angry with him that I had stopped sobbing and crying, aware that he had been deriving too much satisfaction from it to suit me.

When we arrived at the police station, we were put in a waiting room that was filled nearly to capacity with drunks, juvenile delinquents, and prostitutes. I sat down on a bench beside a drunk all slouched over with his chin resting on his chest who was trying to sing "Yankee Doodle." He would sing a while, then weep a while. I sat there for an hour and a half before I was finally told to go to another room.

"Miss Starr, if you would come this way, we will take your picture," a young police officer said.

"A picture? My God, it's a heck of a time to talk about taking a picture. Just look at me. I've been crying, my makeup is smeared, and my hair's a mess," I replied.

"That's okay, we've got to have your picture. It's policy. It's a formality. Stand on the spot, and face the camera," he ordered.

I walked over and stood in front of a blank wall and forced a smile just before he snapped the shutter.

"Dammit, don't smile. I want a serious picture," he barked as he snapped my picture again. "Now I want a profile."

I turned, put my hand on my hip, leaned my head back, and stuck out my chest, just as I had always done for side profiles taken by New York photographers who did publicity portraits for the burlesque trade.

The policeman, irked, ordered, "Pull your chest in, madam. I am only interested in your face!"

"Oh, I guess I don't understand what you mean when you say side profile. I thought you wanted a shot of my bosom."

"Don't get smart with me, lady!"

"Excuse me. You sound just like the Cisco Kid!"

"Who are you calling the Cisco Kid?" he demanded.

"Your captain. Doesn't everyone call him the Cisco Kid? He looks and acts just like him," I replied.

The young policeman stared at me and shook his head as he led me to another room to take my fingerprints.

By the time the bondsman arrived with Manny Jenkins, I was so tired and distressed that I hardly knew where I was. Fortunately, I did not have to spend the night in jail.

The next morning, the Philadelphia radio stations broadcast the story that the panther girl had been arrested by Captain Frank Rizzo without her panther. However, the charges were dropped at the hearing because there was no statute to cover my arrest. Furious with the judge, Rizzo turned and pointed his finger at me as he left the room and threatened, "I'll get you before you leave the city of Philadelphia."

9

For quite a spell after that, I continued to work at the Black Cat Club. The publicity I had gotten served to make the crowds grow larger, and many evenings people were lined up for a block trying to get in. Captain Rizzo continued to make arrests of other strippers throughout the city. Usually when he came into a club, it meant that the strippers were certain to be arrested. It was always the same pattern. He would blow his whistle until it would almost pierce your ears. The club owners were concerned that eventually he would be able to close them all down. But the whistles began to be kind of a thing with the customers. It was considered a real treat to be present when a raid occurred. The audience enjoyed the police captain's antics as much as they did the strippers. Everyone in the City of Brotherly Love was talking about the Cisco Kid.

Three weeks after my first arrest, I saw Captain Rizzo enter the Black Cat Club. My immediate thought was that I would be arrested again. This time, however, he merely stood at the back of the room and watched me perform. I was doing identically the same act as during my previous arrest. When I finished, he walked up to the edge of the stage, placed his hand on my shoulder, and said, "Come here, you. I want to talk to you. I want to talk to you downstairs." He knew that the dressing room was downstairs.

"I don't want to talk to you," I answered.

"Get downstairs," he ordered.

Without further resistance, I walked towards the dressing room. He trailed closely behind. I was dressed in a negligée that I had put on immediately after my act. We went into the dressing room, and he closed the door behind him and sat down in one of the chairs.

I began to gather up my clothing and asked if he would be so kind as to excuse himself while I dressed.

He said, "You don't have to be in a hurry."

"Are you going to take me to jail?"

"No, no. I don't have any intentions of taking you to jail. I just wanted to talk to you. You know, you seem to be different from these other girls."

"No, I'm just the same. I'm just as filthy and obscene as anybody in this whole damn city."

"I didn't say that. That's not what I said about you. Now you calm down."

I sat on a chair across from him without making any further effort to clothe my practically naked body. He began asking all sorts of questions about prostitution, about the club owner, Manny Jenkins, and about other strippers around the city whom I might know. I told him I was not aware of any wrongdoing by any of the people to whom he referred.

As I parried his questions, he grew somewhat restless and began to get irritated. "Come on, now, why don't you level with me?" he asked, staring constantly at my bosom. "I am going to ask you one more time. Are any of the girls selling it?"

"How do you think I would know that?" I demanded. "Are you selling it?"

I was infuriated. "You get the hell out of here! Right now! What kind of woman do you take me for? I don't have to talk to you. Get out!"

He left the room, saying, "Okay. Okay. I'll talk to you later."

I did not answer but slammed the door behind him.

Two nights later, Rizzo came back to the club alone and hauled me off stage right in the middle of my act. "You are under arrest. Get dressed!" he yelled.

He waited outside my dressing room while I changed. This time I did not cry. He put me in his car. This time there was no patrolman driving. Instead of taking me to jail, Rizzo drove around the city himself, talking.

"Why don't you get out of this stripping business? You know I am going to have to arrest you every time I come in and find you doing all those lewd movements on stage," he said as he adjusted his police radio.

"But I love stripping. Besides, the pay is good, and I need to send money home to help support my younger brothers and sisters."

"That's not the point. I've got to clean up the mess in this city, and I am just telling you ahead of time that you are only going to get hurt."

"Well, I am not quitting, and that's that. If you would leave the strippers alone, the club owners would be willing to make it worthwhile for you," I said.

"Blaze, I'll pretend I didn't hear that. Do you know you just offered me a bribe? And do you know what could happen to you for doing such a thing?"

He pulled the car over to the curb. I sat there quietly while he checked in with the police station. When he hung up the microphone, he glanced over and smiled. I sensed what he was after.

"You want to come to my room?" I made it a question.

"Yeah. Where are you staying?"

"The Rio Hotel on Locust Street."

He had already started the car up, and we were headed in the direction of the Black Cat. "I can't come there. That's where all the strippers stay, and I might be recognized. But I do have a friend who has an apartment nearby. I'll meet you there as soon as you get off work," he said.

"If you don't get me back to the club, I am going to miss my last performance," I replied.

As he let me out in front of the club, he squeezed my hand and said, "See you at three o'clock."

I smiled, "Okay."

Everyone was surprised to see me return and even more astonished when I told them how we just rode around town.

Mr. Goodman extended my contract in Philadelphia, and Captain Rizzo continued to visit the club where I worked. The arrests at Philadelphia strip clubs slackened, and things calmed down at the Black Cat. Manny Jenkins was happy. I felt pretty good myself, except for the times when I got to thinking about Carroll and our nice home I wasn't seeing much of.

All through this period, I was constantly trying to invent new acts that would appeal to the audience. One night I had this wild dream that Rizzo and I were in an Indian tent. I was lying on a couch of animal skins and furs. He was an Indian chief in full headdress and was dancing around in the tent. He paid no attention to my seductive gestures but continued just to dance and dance around the tent until suddenly my couch started burning. Smoke and fire were coming up everywhere. Then I finally got him down on the furs and skins with me, and the whole tent went up.

I awakened abruptly and immediately jumped out of bed and jotted down some notes about the dream so I could recall it the next morning. However, when I attempted to reconstruct my notes, none of my jottings seemed to make any sense. I continued to look at the piece of paper, however, and about a week later the entire dream suddenly came back to me. The more I thought of the dream, the more I thought about attempting to develop some sort of act from it. But Captain Rizzo had already made a lot of rules about the club owners not using suggestive props with the strippers, so I knew I could not get away with the skins or the tent on stage.

Still I did not give up on the idea. One day I went to a used furniture store and bought an old beat-up chair without a back. It looked more or less like a hassock. Then, from a magic shop, I purchased a chemical that would make smoke. I sewed a red velvet cover for the chair and placed the smoke-making chemical in a can at the back of it where I could light it with a match. When it was ignited, the entire club seemed to be on fire. The act went well with my name.

The first night I tried it, the audience went wild with laughter. But when I attempted to use the new act a second time, Captain Rizzo was suddenly in the club and in a rage. He rushed to the stage, shouting, "I heard about all the smoke in here last night. What the hell are you doing now? Goddammit, you won't let well enough alone. Don't you use that on stage!"

"Where in the law book does it say that I can't use a hassock to undress on?" I shouted back.

"It doesn't say anything about a hassock," he thundered. "But you . . . you know what you're doing. You're promoting an idea that you're so hot up there the goddamn stage is exploding."

We stood just off the stage arguing back and forth for about ten minutes. I told him about my dream, and his reply was, "You didn't dream that. You're trying to con me, and it's not going to work. If I let you use that, all the other girls are going to be dreaming up crazy props. You've got to get rid of it,'' he ordered.

Surprisingly, he did not arrest me but instead pulled me behind him to the dressing room. "What in the hell are you trying to do? Don't you ever argue in public with me. My God, Blaze, don't you know it will make people think I am having an affair with you?'' He was furious.

I began crying.

"Come on, now, I didn't say that to make you cry,'' he said. He walked over and put his arm around me and tried to console me. "All I was trying to tell you is that I have a future here in Philadelphia, and I can't let you spoil it. Do you understand that?''

I shook my head yes, and he dried my eyes with his handkerchief. I understood all right, but it was my future that interested me.

And now that I had the smoke, I decided that I was going to get the fire. Next day, I went downtown and bought a little settee about two feet wide and four feet long and cut a hole in the top. Next I bought an electric fan and a piece of screen wire and rigged up a switch on the settee that I could use to turn the fan on. The fan would blow a bright piece of Chinese silk up through the hole in the settee to simulate flame. As it did, I would ignite the chemical, and smoke would also start coming up through the hole. As a crowning touch, I attached colored lights to the settee that would flicker when I pulled another switch. My plan was to lie down on the settee and undress in the midst of this pretend conflagration.

As expected, the very first night that I attempted my new act, Captain Rizzo walked in—right in the middle of it. I saw him as he entered the door, and I figured that if he was ever going to arrest me again, he would have to this time. Just as he was halfway up the club room, I flipped the switches. The fan started blowing the ''blaze'' up through the hole in the settee, the lights flickered, and as I touched a match to the chemical, smoke started pouring in every direction.

Rizzo actually thought the place was on fire and yelled at the top of his voice, "Everybody out! Everybody out!"

I burst into laughter. The Cisco Kid ran to the stage, roaring, "What have you done now? Get off there!"

"I will not!" I countered. "The only way you'll get me off this stage is to take me off."

"Stop it, Blaze. You're making an ass out of me," he hissed beneath his breath so nobody would hear. "You know damn well I'll have to take you in because you're defying me in front of these people."

To keep from making matters worse, I agreed to go with him. However, when he started to take my electrified settee off the stage, I protested loudly. "What are you taking my couch for? You're the one that's going to make an ass out of yourself. That's my property. I worked a week on that couch."

At the last instant, he decided to leave it. But he hustled me outside and put me in a police cruiser parked in front of the club. There was another policeman driving the car, and Rizzo and I did not talk on the way to the station. As we drove in stony silence, I got madder and madder. If he arrested me and tried to put me in jail, I would tell everything, I decided. We arrived at the station house, and, sure enough, he booked me. But once again a bondsman was there to go my bail.

Next morning, a lot of newspaper people turned up for the hearing. Captain Rizzo outlined the charge against me. It was wearing indecent clothing. Rizzo insisted that the bikini bottom was different this time from what it had been in previous stripping cases. He told the judge that it had a see-through back and explained that he had kept the evidence the night before to use in court. In an effort to make his point more meaningful to the judge, he walked over to a table where he took a pencil and with it picked up the bikini bottom with the see-through rear. He carried it dangling from the pencil over to the judge's stand and held it up in the air for everyone to see.

"Look at him!" I shouted. "The Cisco Kid's scared he'll get his fingers dirty. Boy, you're not usually afraid to touch those pants! Especially if I'm wearing them! What the hell makes you afraid to touch them now?"

Manny Jenkins grabbed me and held his hand over my mouth. The judge pounded his gavel and said, "Order in the court."

Rizzo ignored me and continued to present his evidence. The case was dismissed despite Rizzo's arguments, but I had had enough of the captain.

"Don't you ever speak to me again, Cisco Kid," I snapped as I walked past him on the way out of the courtroom.

That same evening I called Mr. Goodman and asked him to book me in another city. I was tired of Captain Rizzo riding to fame on my G-string.

10

In January 1959, I arrived at the New Orleans airport from Miami, where I had been working at the Gaiety Night Club. I was in a state of considerable anticipation. José Martinez, the manager of the Sho-Bar on Bourbon Street, had caught my act in Florida a month earlier and offered me $1,000 a week and a year's contract. The chance for a long-term engagement, and at those wages, was just what I needed.

My separation from my husband, Carroll, had been a fact for some time now, though I had not done anything about getting a divorce, and neither had he. Our marriage had been on the brink ever since I had worked at the Black Cat in Philadelphia, and I guess it had been obvious from the very beginning that my career was going to cause us problems. But I had hoped we could handle them, and it still hurt that we hadn't. By 1959, however, I was at the peak of a career that just seemed to go on getting more exciting all the time. Mr. Goodman kept getting offers from the best strip clubs and burlesque houses all over the United States. I had danced at the Casino in Boston and been a big hit with all the boys from Harvard College. I had played the Follies in San Francisco, the Gay Paree in Pittsburgh, and the Continental at 127 W. 52nd Street in Manhattan, among others. They all went for Blaze Starr.

But Bourbon Street was something special. Every girl in the business wanted to strip there. It turned out to be everything I had ever heard it was. Bars and clubs lined both sides of the street. It was a place where night never ended. And the Sho-Bar itself was one of the largest clubs I had ever worked in. It seated almost five hundred people and was always filled to capacity with tourists, sightseers, and the locals who frequent all the clubs along Bourbon Street.

Three nights after I began dancing at the Sho-Bar, a short, stocky, gray-haired man and an entourage of policemen walked into the club. I was in the middle of my act. I figured there was going to be a raid, and I would be hauled off to jail again. By this time, I had been arrested in practically every town that I performed in. It had become sort of a habit with me. There was no reason to believe it would be different in New Orleans. But nothing happened. I finished my act uninterrupted and gave a final wave to the audience before heading for my dressing room. The gray-haired man and the policemen, who were sitting at a table about thirty feet from the stage, applauded vigorously as I left the stage, and I was especially struck by the fact that the gray-haired man stood up and applauded. I found this behavior to be quite strange. I had never been applauded by a policeman or anybody who was with a policeman before.

I had scarcely sat down in my dressing room when the manager, José, knocked on the door. He was all smiles. "The crowd loves you, Blaze. You're going to be great for the Sho-Bar."

I politely thanked him for the compliment and asked him to come in and chat. He said he was sorry, he was in a hurry and had only stopped by to give me a message. "The governor wants to meet you," he said.

I made a face at him.

"I'm not kidding, Blaze," José said. "The governor wants to meet you. He's waiting for you at his table."

I didn't believe it. It didn't make sense—a governor wanting to meet me. "Governors don't go to strip joints," I thought out loud.

"You don't know our governor," said José. "Our governor frequents all the night clubs. He is the biggest fan that the strippers have in New Orleans, and he is a frequent customer at the Sho-Bar. I don't know whether you noticed him, but he's the short, gray-haired man with the policemen."

"Noticed him! Hell, when I saw that bunch walk in, I figured I was going to be arrested. Remind me to tell you about Philadelphia sometime. And some other towns. Anyway, I had no idea that little guy was a governor."

"Well, you don't have to worry about him. Our governor won't take you to jail. And like I say, he's waiting on you."

"My God, I don't know what to say to him. I've never met a governor."

"Look, Blaze, just act yourself. Just go on out there and say hello to him. You're supposed to say 'Mr. Governor' or 'Your Honor,' or something like that. But just be normal. Everything's all right. Evidently he likes you, or he wouldn't have wanted to meet you."

I hurriedly put on my gown and retouched my makeup. Then I took two or three deep breaths and followed José to the governor's table. As I approached the table, the three state policemen and the governor jumped to their feet. The three state policemen stood erect, holding their hats.

"Your Honor, I would like for you to meet Blaze Starr," José said.

The governor reached to shake hands. He was dressed in a loose-fitting blue suit, and his tie was pulled loose from his neck. His white shirt was unbuttoned at the top.

"I'm mighty pleased to meet you, Mr. Governor," I said. "You are the first governor I have ever had the honor to meet."

He introduced me to his chauffeur, Sergeant Ollie Butler, and to the two other policemen, who I assumed were bodyguards. He then offered me a seat, and I sat down beside him. José excused himself and went on about his business. I was probably visibly nervous about being in the presence of such a powerful individual. I still couldn't believe it.

"You know, Miss Starr, it was just an accident that we came in here tonight," he said. "We were on our way to Baton Rouge, but I told Sergeant Butler that I'd just as soon forget about the meeting we had planned to have up there, and I thought maybe we'd just go over to the Sho-Bar and catch some of the stripping acts. And we walked in right in the middle of your act. Of course, we all thought you was just great, and I told the boys here that I thought I'd have you come back, and we'd get acquainted. Where you from, honey?"

"Well, I'm originally from West Virginia."

"West Virginia! Well, I'll be darned. Whereabouts in West Virginia?"

"It's a little isolated place out in the country about 120 miles south of Charleston, the state capital. I know you've never heard of it. It's called Wilsondale. It's on a creek called Twelve Pole Creek."

"Well, well. It sounds like that's the kind of place I'd like. You know, down deep I'm just an old country boy

114

myself. So I guess we've got that much in common anyway, haven't we?''

"Well, I must admit, Wilsondale is way out in the country."

"Say, West Virginia is a fine state. I know a few of your boys up there, like ex-Governor William Marland and, let's see . . . oh yeah, a fellow by the name of Wally Barron. Of course, I reckon your state's gone down a bit now since they elected that Republican, Cecil Underwood. Tell me, what do you think of our great state of Louisiana, and especially New Orleans?''

"I've only been here three or four days, Mr. Governor, but I'll tell you, it's one exciting place."

"Look, Miss Starr, you don't have to call me 'Governor.' All my friends just call me Earl, and I'd probably feel a little more comfortable if you just called me Earl like all my friends do. And, if you don't mind, I'll just call you Blaze.''

He made me feel at ease immediately, and I replied, "Well, that's good. That's the way I like it, too."

We sat there and chatted for almost an hour until it came time for me to do my second act. I told the governor that it was time to leave and that I had certainly been pleased to meet him and would look forward to seeing him again sometime.

He stood up and held my arm as I rose from my chair. "Miss Blaze, it certainly was a pleasure to meet you. And me and the boys are going to sit around and catch your second act. Then I reckon we'll just have to wander off for the evening. But I'll be back."

I hurried on to my dressing room and began preparing for my second performance. He was certainly a kind and gentle man, I thought, as I sat there and did my face. I remembered my daddy talking about his brother Huey Long and something about his being killed by some politicians or something. Earl had mentioned Huey's name during our conversation and said that he was the best governor, next to him, of course, that Louisiana had ever had.

After my second performance, I was chatting with some of the other girls at the club and telling them how exciting it had been to meet the governor.

One of them said, "Well, honey, that ain't nothing. We've all met the governor."

"Yeah, that ain't nothing here, meeting the governor. Every stripper on Bourbon Street has met the governor. He visits all the strip joints. So don't get carried away and think you're something special."

I was surprised at how they could talk about the governor as if he were just an ordinary man. To me he was something special, someone to be respected.

Two nights later, I was in my dressing room preparing to do my first performance when a message was delivered to me that Governor Earl Long was out front and wanted me to join him again after my act. I sent word back that I would be happy to accept his invitation.

As I performed that evening, I looked around in hopes of spotting his table. At the Sho-Bar it was difficult sometimes to see the audience because of the stage lights. However, I sighted Governor Long to the far right. He was sitting there with the state policemen and two or three other strippers at his table. Although he appeared to be carrying on a conversation, he was at the same time watching my act very closely. I caught his eye and threw him a kiss. To my amazement, he stood up and began applauding. Then he turned to his table and motioned for the policemen to stand up, and they too began applauding. They stood there and clapped harder and harder until my act was completed, and I threw them all a second kiss as I left the stage.

I was in my dressing room only four or five minutes before I was dressed and ready to go out to the governor's table. The other girls had left. He stood up again, same as he had done two nights before, and he was dressed pretty much the same way. He extended his hand and said, "Miss Blaze, you were just wonderful, just absolutely wonderful! I've seen all the strippers down here in New Orleans, and you've got them all beat, believe me."

Sergeant Butler and the other two policemen nodded their approval. I sat down, and we chatted once again, mostly small talk. Occasionally, he would say something to Sergeant Butler about politics or about some individual in the legislature, things I didn't know anything at all about. But for the most part we just chatted back and forth. He talked quite a bit about his early childhood and the hard times he experienced when he was a young man.

I had sat there with him for almost an hour when he astounded me by asking me to have dinner with him the following evening at his suite in the Roosevelt Hotel.

"You want me to have dinner with you tomorrow evening?"

"Yes, indeed, Miss Blaze, if you can work it. I always enjoy the company of a beautiful woman. Your first performance isn't until 9:30, and I thought we could have dinner around seven o'clock, and then I would have my chauffeur drive you over here in time for your first performance. How about it? Incidentally, I've already invited several other old friends and acquaintances. I just don't like to eat alone."

"Why. I would be most delighted to have dinner with you."

"Fine! If you'll give me your address, I'll have my limousine come over and pick you up around, let's say, 6:30 tomorrow evening."

"That will be fine," I replied as I borrowed his pen to

scribble down my address on a piece of paper. I handed him the paper, and he read it aloud.

He said, "Why, yes. That's just about, oh, eight or ten blocks from here, isn't it?"

"Yes."

He handed the note to Sergeant Butler and instructed him to pick me up the following evening at 6:30. Sergeant Butler was an extremely well-mannered individual and appeared to be very close to the governor, not only as a servant, but as a friend as well.

After my last performance that night, I sat down and wrote my mother a very lengthy letter and told her all about meeting Governor Earl Long and about his invitation to have dinner with him at the Roosevelt Hotel. I knew this would be exciting to my parents—their daughter having dinner with the governor of Louisiana. It would really be something for them to talk about back on Twelve Pole Creek.

Early the next day, I made an appointment with my hair dresser and had my hair done at three in the afternoon. For the occasion I selected a low-cut, green gown. I must have spent more than two hours getting dressed. At 6:30, the governor's big black limousine pulled up in front of the apartment house. Sergeant Butler escorted me to the car, and I sat down in the spacious back seat.

Within minutes, he parked in front of the Roosevelt Hotel in downtown New Orleans. He motioned to a bell-hop and requested that he escort me to the governor's suite. The bellhop led me through the huge lobby to the elevator. Once the elevator door closed, he looked around at me and grinned. "You a friend of the governor?" he asked.

I replied, "Yes." It was the first time anyone had asked me that question, and it was a real good feeling to be able to say that I was a friend of the governor.

"Best governor the state of Louisiana has ever had,"

the bellhop said. "He's done more for my people than any other governor ever thought about doing, including his brother Huey. He's the only governor that's ever been decent to us colored people. My folks vote for him all the time."

I smiled at him as the elevator stopped. He led me down the corridor and knocked on the door of the governor's suite. Governor Long answered the door himself. "I was expecting you, Miss Blaze. I knew that was you. Come in and meet my friends."

He introduced me to four or five older couples whom he had invited to dinner. "Let me get you something to drink. What would you like?"

"Scotch and soda," I replied.

"Bring her a scotch and soda," he yelled at one of the waiters and right away half whispered to me, "You know, I can't drink any hard stuff. I've got a bad stomach. The most powerful stuff I drink is a Coca-Cola." He held up a bottle of Coke from which he was drinking. "Of course, as far as I'm concerned, Miss Blaze, they've never made anything that tastes any better than a Coke anyway."

His guests looked to be mostly people about the same age as the governor. All the women had on long gowns, but none of their dresses were low-cut like mine. I felt a little out of place, and I also found it a little difficult to carry on a conversation. When Earl left the room for a few minutes, I found myself engaged in small talk with two of the guests. One of them asked my profession.

I started to say that I was a stripper but had second thoughts and decided to be a little more formal. "I'm in show business."

"Oh, you are an actress?"

"No, I . . . I am a dancer."

"Ballet?"

"No, I'm an exotic dancer. I perform at the Sho-Bar."

The women did not seem upset that I was a stripper, and we continued with our conversation.

Earl finally came back into the room carrying four bottles of Worcestershire sauce, proclaiming happily that no one had ever eaten real good chicken à la king until they had eaten it the way he prescribed. I soon learned that he had ordered chicken à la king for all the guests. Instead of letting the waiter do it, he himself placed the four bottles of Worcestershire sauce around the large table that had been brought in moments earlier.

It was a fun evening. I sat at the head of the table with Earl, and we all had chicken à la king, Governor Long-style. It was smothered with Worcestershire sauce. But he was right. It was extremely tasty.

The governor was interrupted several times by an aide who kept coming in and whispering in his ear. Each time, Earl barked out a few orders, and the aide would leave. I could hear the continuous ringing of the telephone in the next room.

After dinner, the guests gradually excused themselves until finally there was no one left but me. The governor walked over to where I was sitting and said, "Well, let's see, we still have an hour or so to go before I have to take you to the Sho-Bar. I sure wish you didn't have to work tonight; we'd go see the town."

I was a little bit puzzled by his statement and asked, "You mean you would take me out to all the clubs?"

He replied, grinning, "There's nothing I would like more than that."

"But wouldn't you be afraid that people would see us?"

"Oh, I don't worry about things like that. Everybody sees Old Earl, and they're always talking about something or another anyway."

"But what about your wife? You are married, aren't you?"

"Honey, I'm married. Me and Miz Blanche live in a big mansion; but she lives on one end, and I live on the other, and we haven't slept together in over two years. You might say it's just a marriage in name only. What about you?" he asked. "Are you married?"

"Well, I'm married, but I'm going through quite an ordeal at the present time. My husband and I are in the process of getting a divorce. I shouldn't be talking about such private matters, though. I'm sure you're not interested in things like that."

"Oh, but I am," he was fast to reply. "Come on, let's go over here and sit down, and I'll let you tell me about it."

"Well, there's really nothing to tell about. I've just run into a lot of problems with my husband."

"I tell you what, Miss Blaze, I think everybody needs somebody to talk to when they've got problems. How long have you been married?"

"A little over five years, I guess. The first couple years were absolutely beautiful. Everything that my husband, Carroll, and I had planned turned out for us. Shortly after we were married, I went on tour across the country—Philadelphia, Boston, New York, San Francisco, Los Angeles, Miami. You name the city, and I've been there.

"I guess my husband first got jealous when I was working in Philadelphia. He got jealous of a police captain by the name of Frank Rizzo. One of the girls at the club where I was working called Carroll and told him a lot of things. From there on, the marriage started going downhill. We would quarrel and make up, quarrel and make up. But even with all the problems, we loved each other very much, and I thought the marriage was on the road to recovery when I went to work in Miami, just before coming to New Orleans. I was sending Carroll money to help remodel the Club Diamond, which we own in Baltimore, and everything seemed to be settling down once again.

"While I was working in Miami, I met a young girl who wanted to become a stripper. She was a beautiful, blond Canadian. In a very short while, I taught her everything I knew about stripping. She really became good in a hurry. So I called Carroll and asked him if he would like to have a beautiful stripper in the Club Diamond. I felt it would be good for his business. He agreed, so I told him all about her. You know, I even gave her her stage name. I won't tell you what it is. It still upsets me too much to think about, and you might meet her some day, you liking strip acts the way you do. Anyway, Carroll was excited with the idea and arranged to meet her at the airport two days later. He even had a big sign erected out front—"Blaze Starr's protégé"—and then her name that I thought up.

"Two weeks later, I went back home to Baltimore, and one of my neighbors called me and told me that there had been a woman living in the house while I was gone. I naturally became furious and confronted Carroll. He denied everything and said there certainly had been no woman living in the house while I had been gone. However, I made a few other inquiries and determined without a doubt that my protégé had been living with my husband in my own home."

I stopped talking, aghast that I had poured my heart out to somebody I hardly knew—and a governor, at that. "Earl, I don't know what's the matter with me. I shouldn't be sitting her telling you about all my problems."

"No, no, don't feel that way," he said as he reached over and patted me on the knee. "Human beings are the most interesting things in the world. And I love to hear people talk about themselves, especially if it's somebody I like. It helps me to understand them. Go ahead, tell me the rest of it," he urged.

"Well, I'm really ashamed to tell you the rest of it, but I guess it won't hurt anything. You know, you're the first person I will have ever told this to. And I never dreamed that I would be sitting here telling this story to the governor of the state of Louisiana. It doesn't make sense."

Earl smiled. "Well, I put my pants on just like everybody else. Being the governor is not all that much. Besides, listening to other people's problems helps me take my mind off all my activities and all my own problems."

"Well, I confronted Carroll again, and this time he admitted it. I really felt betrayed knowing that the young girl I had helped so much would do a thing like that to me. And I guess my ego was hurt a little bit, too. I just never dreamed that Carroll would ever look at another woman, no matter what anybody reported to him about me.

"We agreed immediately to a separation and began making plans for a divorce. Carroll told me that I could go ahead and make all the legal arrangements, and he would go along with whatever I was able to work out. And I guess everything would have been over with there, but this girl started calling me on the phone, telling me that Carroll loved her and had never loved me. And the more she called, the more furious I became with her.

"She was still stripping at the Club Diamond, and one afternoon when she called me, I decided that I was going to get revenge. I planned, along with my sister Faye, to go to the Club Diamond and just beat the hell out of her. That's what they do in West Virginia when some woman tries to steal another woman's husband. They just catch them out and beat the hell out of them.

"I was still good friends with Angelo, Carroll's brother, so I had him call me when Carroll left the club. When Faye and I got to the club, this little blonde traitor had just finished her dance and had gone to the dressing room. I guess it was all sort of unfair, but Faye held her, and I lit into her like a circle saw. I beat the hell out of her.

After it was all over with, I felt ashamed of myself for what I had done. But it's water over the dam, I guess. I still haven't gotten the divorce, but I plan to very soon. I think I'll go to Mexico. That's where we went on our honeymoon, so I kind of hate to, but they tell me you can get a divorce down there in a day's time."

Earl had listened with interest all through my story. "Well, I guess we all have our problems," he said. "My marriage has been very miserable. My wife, Miz Blanche, is one of these high-society women. She's all the time telling me how to dress and what I should do and what I shouldn't do. And it just really gets on my nerves. I like to do what I like to do, and I don't like anybody telling me what I have to do. I was brought up in the country, and I don't guess I ever adjusted to all these highfalutin customs you're supposed to go through. I guess I'm a common man, and I like common people. How long have you been stripping, Blaze?"

"Well, let's see, it's been almost ten years now. I've been all over the country, in practically every major city. You know, I even made a movie once."

"Is that right?"

"Well, it was a nudist movie."

Earl chuckled and raised an eyebrow.

"Yeah, that was the other time Carroll almost left me. He became very very furious when he found out what I was going to do. But you see, this company offered me $10,000, and we needed the money. I just couldn't turn it down. He was afraid all of his friends in Baltimore would see it. It wasn't really that bad. It was called *Nature Girl,* and I wore a bikini bottom all the way through it. Most of the shots were of my breasts. I don't think I had ever seen Carroll that mad before. But he calmed down after two or three days. Besides, I promised him I would quit working after the movie was completed. But, you know, I really just couldn't. I love stripping. It's no wonder he stepped out on me, I guess, the way I treated him.''

Earl and I sat there and talked for another thirty minutes or so. I continued to tell him all about my past, and he continued to tell me about himself. We both agreed that it had been a most enjoyable evening, and he promised that he would invite me over again soon for dinner.

By the time I got back to the Sho-Bar, I was fifteen minutes late for my act. I apologized to José. A big smile spread over his face. He winked and said, ''I understand. Don't worry about it.''

11

Earl and I saw each other as much as possible that winter. His job as governor kept him busy, but we always managed to get together at least once a week. Sometimes it was dinner at the Roosevelt Hotel, but most of the time it was an hour or two at the Sho-Bar between my performances.

At Earl's suggestion, I moved to the Flamingo Motel in late February. It was a very private place on the outskirts of town, and he knew the owner. If he wanted to visit with me there, it would be unlikely that anyone would see him. I **was** concerned, however, that some reporter would discover our relationship and attempt to make something bad out of it. I often talked to Earl about the situation, but he assured me that there was no problem and that I should not worry about it.

I had two rooms at the Flamingo Motel—one for myself and one for my younger sister Debbie, who was also stripping at the Sho-Bar. Debbie had left Twelve Pole Creek three or four years earlier and had traveled with me from club to club throughout the United States. I had taught her all she needed to know about stripping, and she became very good. Another of my sisters, Faye, also had learned stripping but was uncomfortable with it and soon gave it up. Debbie loved the life of the clubs as much as I did. During the past two years, we had always arranged to get engagements at the same places.

One evening in early March, Earl came into the Sho-Bar and asked me to go with him the following day on a trip out in the backwoods. He had told me earlier that he was planning to run for governor again and that he just wanted to get up north to see how the "boys" felt about it. I told him that I would just be in the way, but he was adamant. He said it would be a good opportunity for me to see the rural side of Louisiana and added that if we had time he would like for me to see his little farm, which he called the Pea Patch. It was located at Winnfield, a small town in Winn Parish. I consented, and he said he would have his limousine pick me up the following morning at 7 A.M. at the Flamingo.

I had hardly finished breakfast when Earl's chauffeur came into the restaurant for me. It was a beautiful day outside. There was a slight breeze, and the sun was shining brightly. According to the forecast, the temperature was supposed to reach the low eighties. When we walked outside, Earl was standing beside the limousine holding his white hat in one hand and blowing his nose with the other. He was still in the same jovial mood as he had been the night before.

Within minutes, we were outside the city limits of New Orleans and headed towards the back country. As we traveled, I discovered that some of the roads of Louisiana were almost as bad as the road on Twelve Pole Creek. The countryside, however, was entirely different. Instead of the big lush mountains like we had in West Virginia, everything was sort of flat and swampy. In its own way, it was still very beautiful.

We drove for more than three hours before we arrived at Earl's scheduled meeting in Colfax, a tiny town almost directly north of Baton Rouge and several miles south of the Pea Patch. I stayed in the limousine during the entire session, and Earl was back within thirty or forty minutes with a big grin on his face. His comment on the meeting was that everything here was "tied up as tight as a fiddle string" and that he had everything sewed up in the Eighth District.

Earl told me that the votes out here in the country were just as important as the votes in the city and that his strength as a politician had always come from the poor people and the Negroes. He told me that he was going to get a law passed in the legislature that would enable more colored people to vote in the upcoming primary election. He was constantly talking politics, and I made every effort to understand what was really happening in the state. But I had never been very politically minded, and it was difficult for me to understand all that was going on behind the scenes. Anyway, Earl convinced me that he was going to be the next governor and that there wasn't anyone who would have a chance of beating him.

He had decided against going to the Pea Patch, claiming that it would take an entire day to go that far. Instead, we headed back towards New Orleans. We had the radio on full blast, and the chauffeur almost didn't hear Earl when he told him to pull over at a little country store that must have been forty or fifty miles south of Colfax. Eight or ten black folks were sitting around on the front porch and when the limousine stopped, they all raised up. Earl was outside shaking hands almost before the car had a chance to come to a complete halt. Everyone seemed to recognize him immediately. We all followed Earl inside the store. He walked over and called the store owner by his first name, shook hands, and began chatting. The place reminded me of the store that Old Man Marcum had on Twelve Pole Creek. There were lard cans, sacks of pinto beans, and barrels of rice cluttering up the interior of the store. A large counter ran from one end to the other, and two drop cords on which light sockets were fastened hung down from the ceiling.

Soon a lot of other people started coming into the store, and kids came out of every crack and corner. Earl grabbed a candy jar off the counter, opened it, and started passing out candy to all the kids. It was as if they knew in advance what he was going to do. Before we left, he bought every ham in the store and passed them out to everyone who came in the front door. He also bought two onions, a loaf of bread, an assortment of potted meat and crackers, and a case of Coca-Cola. By the time he got through talking, we had spent more time at the store meeting people than he had spent at the political meeting.

Earl chuckled as he got back in the car. "If it weren't for the niggers down here, the Longs wouldn't have a chance in politics. Of course, you know me and my brother Huey have always done more for the niggers than anybody else in the whole South. You know, Blaze," he continued, "it's a shame how the niggers have been treated anyway, and we're going to have to realize sooner or later that they're just like everybody else, that they've got a soul and they'll go to heaven. And sooner or later, we're going to have to live with them. Of course, if I went out and said that publicly, I wouldn't get a vote among the white people. Anyway, they know what I do for them. Right now a nigger ain't got a chance hardly in this state. They can challenge his right to vote and prevent him from being registered. But you just wait and see what I do this coming May. I'm going to have the legislature pass a state law that's going to make it easier for them to vote. But I'm going to have a hell of a lot of opposition."

He continued to talk about the upcoming election and how he was going to maneuver to get himself re-elected. He explained that the state constitution did not allow a governor to succeed himself but that he had figured out a way to get around it. He would resign before the election, and the lieutenant governor would be appointed governor to serve the remainder of the term. He could run again because he would be succeeding the lieutenant governor rather than himself. He added that the state supreme court would have to make a final ruling on his plan but that he didn't think that would be any great problem. Most of the court members owed him a political debt of one kind or another, so he felt they would certainly rule in his favor.

A few minutes after we left the store, Earl once again told the chauffeur to pull over beside the road.

"Miss Blaze," he said, "I'm taking you on a picnic."

He took one bag of the groceries that he had bought and gave the other to the chauffeur and the state policeman. He told them to go on up the road and have a picnic of their own, then come back and pick us up in two or three hours. I laughed out loud when I discovered what he was up to. I had been a little curious when he bought the groceries at the store but would never have guessed that he was planning a picnic.

We walked across an open field and into the edge of a patch of woods that contained huge oak trees with moss hanging down from them. They were absolutely beautiful but totally unlike the oaks we had back on Twelve Pole Creek. Earl stopped under a big oak near a small stream.

The temperature had already climbed to a good eighty degrees. I told Earl that it was strange to have such a warm day this early in March, as sometimes back in West Virginia we still had snow at this time of the year. He replied that the weather was always beautiful in Louisiana, except in midsummer when it was very hot and the humidity stayed near 100 per cent.

Earl pulled a couple of Cokes from his pockets, then took out a pocketknife and cut the lid off a small can of pork and beans, being very careful not to cut himself. He opened the potted meat with keys he took from the back of each can, and peeled the onion, and sliced it with his knife before spreading the meat on the crackers. As he spread each sandwich, he reached it to me to hold, and when he finished, he carefully wiped off the knife and put it back into his pocket.

We sat there about thirty minutes, eating the sandwiches, drinking the Coke, which was a little warm but still refreshing, and having a great time enjoying the solitude. When we finished eating, Earl leaned back against the oak tree and pulled my head back against his shoulder.

Looking at the stream of water reminded me of my childhood back on Twelve Pole Creek, and I recalled the many times June and I had slipped off to go skinny-dipping. I asked Earl if he had ever had a similar experience.

He looked around and grinned. "Sure. You tell me a boy that ain't never gone skinny-dipping. When I was growing up, me and the boys always went skinny-dipping. And every now and then, some of the girls would even go with us."

I laughed aloud. "When June and I was cow-hunting, we would sometimes go early in the afternoon, strip off, and just sit under a little waterfall down below the house. The water was ice cold, but it was a lot of fun."

All of a sudden, Earl said, "You want to go skinny-dipping now?"

"You're not serious, are you?"

"Sure. Why not? I dare you," he said.

"I will if you will."

"It's a deal," he replied.

I stripped to my panties and bra and ran towards the stream. Earl was still fumbling with his shirt but finally managed to get the button unfastened on the cuff. He threw it over a bush and pulled off his shoes. He didn't pull off his pants, but simply rolled them above his knees. By that time, I had already entered the water. It wasn't deep, only two or three feet, but it felt great. Earl walked cautiously down to the edge of the bank and stuck his foot in the water.

About that time I looked down and noticed that three or four leeches were sticking to my leg. I became horrified and started screaming. I ran towards Earl as fast as I could. "Look on my leg! Look on my leg!" I howled.

"It's those goddamned leeches. I should have realized it. Just about every stream down here has got the damn things in it," he was saying apologetically. "Don't touch them. Come up here and let me get them off. There's a certain way you've got to do it."

He fumbled through his coat pocket until he found a book of matches, took one out, lit it, and held it to the leeches until they dropped off. Altogether there were five, and within seconds he had removed them all. I felt half sick but also relieved, and we both stood there laughing about the abrupt end to our skinny-dipping until we had dressed.

Earl once again sat down and leaned back against the big tree and pulled me over close to him. He looked at me seriously and said, "Blaze, what would you think if an old man told you that he loved you?"

"If it was the right man, I might tell him that I loved him, too."

He looked at me for a moment, then pulled me up close against him and kissed me. It was a long, passionate kiss, and I was breathless. He repeated, "Blaze, I love you."

"I love you, too, Earl."

He kissed me again, then again. We stretched out in the grass beneath the tree and held hands, looking up through the limbs of the large oak tree at the blue sky. Neither of us spoke for a long time. I kept thinking about how strange it was. Here I was somewhere in Louisiana with the governor, lying out under a big oak tree, in love with a man who was old enough to be my grandfather. But I was not going to worry about that. Other young women loved older men, and why should it be that different for me? The thing that did disturb me was the fact that we were both married, although it was just a matter of time before I would get my divorce.

I had been impressed with Earl from the moment I had met him. However, I had no idea that the relationship would develop to this stage. On the inside, he was a kind, gentle person. On the outside, he was all-powerful, and he made things happen. I had never experienced a dull moment with him from the time we had met at the Sho-Bar. But although it was a beautiful relationship, I knew that by his being governor, such an important position, matters could become very entangled. I had promised that I would never tell anyone about our relationship and had asked him if he could trust his chauffeur and aides. He had assured me that they would never breathe a word of anything to anyone and that there was really nothing to worry about. Besides, he had told me time and time again that he and Miz Blanche could not live together and would already have been separated and divorced had it not been for his being the governor. He was afraid of what it might do to him politically if he divorced her.

We were still lying there under the big oak tree when we heard the limousine horn. Earl looked down and noted that it was almost four o'clock. "Can you believe it?" he said. "We have been here almost four hours."

He stood up first, then helped me to my feet. I was just about as tall as he was, and, as he pulled me up, he embraced me again, kissed me, and told me once again that he loved me. We held hands as we walked across the field to the waiting limousine.

The chauffeur was stretched out in the front seat, and the state policeman was outside the car, walking back and forth. Earl and I slipped into the back seat of the limousine, and he said, "Let's go to New Orleans."

During the following weeks, Earl spent as much time as he could with me at the Flamingo. Usually he would come over around one o'clock in the afternoon and spend three or four hours. He had told me about all the earlier problems he had had with his heart, and the rapid pace at which he lived made me quite concerned about his health. I often talked with him about it, but he kept assuring me that he was a very healthy man. Sometimes when I brought up the subject, it upset him, and he accused me of not really loving him because he was an old man. On one occasion, he even brought pictures of himself as a young man just to show me how handsome he was. I told him that was not necessary, that I loved him for what he was now, not what he was then. This seemed to please him very much.

One afternoon in mid-April when Earl came over to the Flamingo, the heat was absolutely terrible, and the air conditioner at the motel had gone off. He unbuttoned his shirt, and before sitting down on the edge of the bed he got a cold Coke and rolled it back and forth across his face. He loved the feel of the cold bottle, and when it warmed up, he had me get him a fresh one. He drank part of it, then sat there and continued to roll the bottle back and forth across his face. I was as miserable from the heat as he and had stripped to my slip.

Around two o'clock, Earl decided to take an afternoon nap. I told him that would be fine and that while he was sleeping, I would mend a gown I had snagged about a week before and sew on a button that he had popped off his shirt.

He had been asleep for about thirty minutes when I

heard some cars pull up on the outside. That was nothing unusual, however, so I continued to sew the gown. But about five minutes later, there was a horrible crash on the front door. The door flew open, and four men stood there holding a huge crosstie. My screaming and the noise of the men ramming the door woke Earl. Clad only in a pair of shorts, he rushed towards the men, yelling for them to get out.

Outside I heard a woman shout, "You have disgraced me! You have disgraced yourself!"

Earl yelled, "You dirty sons of bitches, get yourselves out of here. You dirty bastards! Take Miz Blanche and get the hell out of here right now, or I'll have every goddamned one of you arrested."

I was horrified. I heard the woman screaming hysterically, but Earl's shouting drowned out whatever she was saying. The four men dropped the crosstie and left the room. Earl kicked the door closed, still cursing at the top of his voice. "That bitch! She doesn't love me; she's never loved me. But every woman I've ever spoken to, she's become jealous of."

He was terribly angry and quite pale. I became concerned about his condition, and, quickly collecting myself, I sat down on the bed and asked him to lie down. He complied, and I got a cold towel and held it to his brow. After a few minutes, the color returned to his face, and he became more composed. He sat up on the bed and began to laugh.

I asked, "What's it all about, Earl? What's happening?"

"Well, I've suspected for some time now that Miz Blanche was having me followed. And now she knows about us for sure."

"Will she let it out?" I asked.

"No, she's not going to tell anybody. She's not going to take a chance on hurting the Long name. She sure is going to give me hell when I get home, though. Don't worry about a thing, though, Blaze. I'll handle this situation. But there's one thing we're going to have to do, and we may as well do it right now. I want you to start in the morning, and I want you to go look for an apartment. And get it up on the second floor. If I go out and start looking, they're going to know exactly where you're staying, so it's better for you to leave here. If you get up on the second floor, they're not going to be breaking in with a log.''

He lay back down on the bed and stretched out. I sat there beside him, thinking about what had just happened. Finally, I looked over at him and said, "Earl, I really don't want to cause you any trouble. Maybe it would be better if we just didn't see each other any more.''

"What are you talking about?'' he asked.

"Well, you've got to realize that you're governor of the state, and you're a married man, and there's not much chance of you being otherwise. And if it were ever to get out publicly that we're seeing each other, it would destroy you politically.''

"Aw, don't worry about a thing like that. There ain't nothing going to get out. Miz Blanche, she'd die and go to hell before she'd say anything about it. It would be too much humiliation for her. Don't worry about it. I'll take care of everything. You just don't worry about a thing.'' He reached over, took my hand, and held it tightly, and assured me that everything would be all right. "I love you, Blaze, and that's that, and that's the way it's going to be. And you love me.''

As I got up from the bed, I bent down and kissed him lightly and squeezed his hand. He smiled, and within minutes he was back asleep. He stayed with me the remainder of the evening, and it was midnight before he left to return to the mansion.

The next day, I followed Earl's advice and rented an apartment in the Esplanade Apartment Building. It was three rooms and located on the second floor, so there wouldn't be any problem with anyone attempting to break the front door down with a crosstie. The building also had two exists, one of them traveling underground for almost a block.

I remained somewhat tense after the incident at the Flamingo Motel and was very cautious about my affair with Governor Long. He sensed this and was constantly assuring me that everything would be all right. About two weeks later, he came by the Sho-Bar one evening during my second performance, and, as soon as I finished, I went over to his table. Before I hardly had a chance to say hello, he reached into his pocket and pulled out a ring.

"Blaze," he asked, "Hon, will you marry me?"

With no hesitation whatsoever, I said, "Yes. Yes, I will."

In front of everyone, he grabbed me and kissed me.

Maybe the Sho-Bar was a rather unromantic place for a marriage proposal, but Earl was a very unusual man, and it was impossible to anticipate what he might do next. No sooner had he proposed and handed me the ring than he asked me to give it back. For an instant, I thought the whole thing was a joke. But he reached into his pocket and pulled out a march larger ring. It must have been at least four carats.

Laughing, he said, "I just wanted to see if you would really marry me if I just gave you this half-carat. But now that I see you're really sincere, I want you to take this real diamond."

Naturally I was pleased with the big diamond. I placed it on my finger and held it up for him to see.

Later in the evening, I told him, "The marriage proposal is all right, but how do you propose to pull it off? You're still a married man, and I haven't got my divorce yet."

"Don't you ever worry about a thing like that. As soon

as I get everything squared away, I'm going to get a divorce from Miz Blanche. Things have been rough as hell ever, since she caught you and me together at the Flamingo. She's been making her brags to some of the help over at the mansion that she's going to do away with me. And to tell you the truth, I wouldn't put it past her.''

He continued to tell me that he had some concern about the food he was eating at the mansion, and he suspected that maybe she was already attempting to put something in the food that would disagree with him. In recent days, he said, he had been having very serious stomach pains. "You know, Blaze,'' he said, "it's a heck of a time for me to be having all these problems, with the legislative session coming up. And if I'm going to run for governor again, I certainly have to get the bill passed that will enable more of the niggers to vote. Anyway, if I can get through this May session of the legislature, and everything works out all right, we can sit down and finalize our plans.

Earl came and went without incident at our new apartment. On several occasions, I would prepare his favorite meal after he went out and bought the ingredients. I had gotten the recipe for chicken à la king from the head chef at the Hotel Roosevelt. Earl always claimed that I could prepare it even better than the chef, but I think he was only kidding. It was a good dish, however, doused with Worcestershire sauce à la Long.

The only thing Earl seemed to enjoy more than his chicken à la king was the weekly manicure and pedicure I gave him. I spent an hour or so at least once a week doing his fingernails and toenails, and he was totally relaxed when I did it.

In early May, Earl came to the apartment one evening very upset. As he sat down on the sofa, he said, "Blaze, I know it's a fact now. They're out to get me, and my own nephew Russell is involved in it with Miz Blanche. What they're afraid of is that my relationship with you is going to destroy the Long name. What they're trying to do is drive me crazy."

He continued, "You know, I've been telling you about these strange feelings I've been having and about the stomach problems. Well, I slipped off yesterday and went to a doctor. He took a blood test and told me that I had all sorts of strange drugs in my system that I shouldn't have. I told him I hadn't taken anything but my regular heart medicine and showed him the pills that had been prescribed for me. But he claimed there was some sort of narcotic that showed up in my blood and said that it had an opposite effect to the heart medicine I am taking. He said the kind of stuff he found in my blood was making me tense. What I think they're trying to do is drive me crazy so they can put me in a mental institution."

I could see that Earl was terribly worried. It became even more evident during the next few days, especially during the legislative session. He told me that I was the only person he trusted, and he stayed with me practically every free minute he had. I watched his performance on television as he went before the legislature, and I saw the disappointment on his face when he failed to get his voting reform bill passed. He took the microphone from one of his opponents and lambasted the legislature for its failure to enact voting reform legislation.

As Earl had previously reasoned, William Rainach, a state senator and potential candidate for the office of governor, was his strongest foe against the bill. At one point, Rainach shouted, "Our registration laws are based not on education but on intelligence, something that is bred into people for thousands of years. It's been bred into the white people of this world." While he was speaking, he was interrupted at the end of almost each sentence by avid supporters who had crammed into the gallery to witness the debate. By the time he finished, I was so mad I could have clawed his eyes out. I knew that Earl must have been even angrier than I was, for occasionally the television cameras would focus on him, and I could tell by his expression that he was upset.

Earl's friend and floor leader in the legislature, Ben Holt, argued for the bill as best he could amidst a howl of hisses and boos from the galleries and floor. "You've got to let them vote. A colored man is still a man—a human being with a soul like you and I have. You can't kick him around like a farm animal."

Earl stood up and interrupted once again. As the television cameras focused on him, he shouted that he meant "the people that sleep with them at night and kick them in the street in the daytime." Again there were jeers and boos from the spectators.

Earl went on to tell about the death of an uncle. "About 1908 I had an uncle who got killed," Earl said as the spectators quieted. "He'd been a good man, good to his family, good to me. Well, he got drunk one night, went down to the colored quarters, kicked a nigger man out of bed, and he got into that bed. That nigger man was so enraged he shot my poor old uncle, and he died. Do you know that's what the colored people resent now most. They want their womenfolk left alone." He went on and on, and the more he talked, the madder he became. No words were spared. He even threw in a little profanity for good measure.

An aide tugged at Earl's coattail, and suddenly Earl calmed down and apologized to a group of Catholic nuns and parochial school children who were seated in the gallery. Raising his arms to the spectators, he said, "Let's me and you swear we won't use any profanity as long as possible."

Joe Waggoner, a representative, also attempted to apologize for Earl's profanity. But he only made matters worse when he turned to Earl and yelled, "I've heard it said you were sick, but since I've been here this morning, I've been able to diagnose you as sick. If I've ever seen a man in my life with constipation of the brain and diarrhea of the mouth, you're that man.''

Earl rushed towards Waggoner as a group of representatives jumped to their feet to restrain him. Earl clenched his fist and yelled, ''I can interrupt that bastard any time I want to.''

One of the bartenders who was watching the debate with me became excited and threw his towel high in the air. ''Give them hell, Earl,'' he said. ''They are all as phony as a three-dollar bill.''

The next day Earl continued his barrage of criticism against the opponents of his bill, and as he left the legislative chamber, he was jeered and booed by many of the legislators and spectators who had packed the halls.

Then it all happened, just as Earl had predicted it would. That same day, Earl's wife, Blanche, his nephew, Russell Long, and several other advisers to the Long family met in the East Room of the mansion and made the decision to commit Earl to a private mental institution outside the state. Hospital attendants were placed in his room where he was held captive until he was flown to Texas the next morning.

12

I was terribly shocked the morning of May 31 when I read in the Baton Rouge *Morning Advocate* that Earl had been taken to Galveston and placed in a mental hospital. I ran to my dressing room and cried. I had been concerned about him anyway, for I had not seen him since he stalked out of the legislative session. The words Earl had spoken weeks before in my apartment rang in my ears. "Blaze, they're going to try to put me away. They are slipping some kind of drug in my food, and it's causing me to become very tense and irritable. They are afraid that I am going to destroy the Long name because of my relationship with you."

For the next few days, I thought about going to the newspapers with my story, but I realized that it might only make matters worse. Senator Russell Long came down from Washington and addressed the state legislature to explain why his uncle had been committed. No one would ever believe a stripper over a U.S. Senator.

My footsteps were hounded by newspaper reporters

and radio and television commentators, however, all wanting me to comment on Earl's condition. They knew the governor and I had been together constantly. But the public did not really know of our relationship, and I decided to remain silent. I was afraid of saying something that would cause even more trouble for Earl, if that were possible. One leading magazine offered me a sizable sum of money for a story. My only story was that I had nothing to say.

However, Blanche Long didn't hesitate to tell her side of the story. As reported in the June 15 issue of *Life* Magazine, she said,

> I knew this was coming eight months ago, it was just as plain as day. Suddenly Earl started talking about running for a fourth term as governor, and it got so that that was all he would talk about. He stopped eating, and even though he had given up smoking years ago because of a thrombosis condition, he started to smoke cigarettes again . . . he couldn't sleep. . . .
>
> I was so sick with worry over him that I called the family together and warned them that we would have to do something or Earl would drive himself to the grave. . . . Last August we started to build a new house, the first one we had ever built on our own. He was all for it at first, but then he started to worry that people would resent his living in such a grand manner. . . . He was called on for several conferences with the Internal Revenue people, and that worried him, too. Every little thing began to build up on his mind until it was obvious that he was getting sicker every day. He even admitted to me that he was a sick man and needed to get away to a hospital for a long rest, but he always had something more important to do.

It got so that I would have to cry myself to sleep at night or hope that sedatives would help me get some rest. I've never taken so many tranquilizers in my life. . . .

He started doing things he had never done before. He made the troopers who drive his car travel at 100 mph where before he had always made them stay down to 55. Everywhere he went he made them run the police siren full blast where before he had forbidden them to use it.

I was outraged at the article. Everyone would now believe Earl was crazy. I wanted so badly to defend him against the claim that he was insane and to tell his side of the story. But my better judgment convinced me to remain silent.

I did know that Earl Long would not roll over and play dead, that he would fight Miz Blanche and Russell Long as long as he had a breath in him. Within two weeks, he was able to free himself from the private institution in Galveston, but only after he agreed not to prosecute Miz Blanche and Russell on charges of kidnapping him. However, as soon as he entered the state of Louisiana, Miz Blanche had him recommitted. Again by force, he was taken to Mandeville, a state mental institution. I bought a copy of the June 29 issue of *Time* magazine to read its account of what Miz Blanche had done to him.

Determined to have her husband committed again, she called . . . the coroner of East Baton Rouge Parish, arranged . . . to get commitment papers ready, then sped up the 80-mile, Huey-built Air Line Highway to Baton Rouge to sign them. . . . Coroner Williams and Parish Sheriff Bryan Clemmons ordered two detectives onto the highway at the parish line to wait for Earl Long who would surely soon be racing for Baton Rouge to reclaim his power.

Sure enough, a half hour later, a white, unlabeled, state-police Ford sped by. A trooper was driving, and with him sat Earl Long. . . .

The detectives pulled abreast of the Ford, waved the driver to the roadside. They greeted the Governor pleasantly, told him that they had been ordered to escort him to the capital. Long's driver got out of the Ford; Chief Detective Herman Thompson slid in behind the wheel and made for Baton Rouge. The disheveled Governor seemed delighted with the attention, spent the remainder of the trip trading small talk.

It was only after Thompson pulled into the basement ramp area of the courthouse at Baton Rouge that Earl Long realized that he had been tricked. "What's going on?" he cried. Thompson told him about the commitment papers. "Goddamn! Goddamn you all," screamed Earl. "You all are doing it again. . . ."

The police tried to get the Governor to leave the car for an interview with three examining doctors. He refused, insisted that the doctors could talk to him in the car. As aides went off to get the doctors, Earl moaned over and over, "Goddamn, all because of a woman, all because of a woman."

I stopped reading. The mention of "a woman" was the first hint that had crept into the press, as far as I knew, of my involvement with Earl. It was odd, because everybody along Bourbon Street and in fact all over New Orleans and Baton Rouge knew, but the newspapers, especially the *Times-Picayune* that was really out to get Earl, I guess didn't have enough evidence at that time to risk writing about us. I felt sick and scared, especially since in the meantime, as the whole mess built to a climax, I had started receiving threatening phone calls at the Sho-Bar. On one such occasion, the caller said, "Miz Blanche has a pair of concrete shoes for you, and if you don't get the hell out of New Orleans immediately, you're going to find yourself in the bottom of the Mississippi River."

"You tell Miz Blanche to go straight to hell!" I answered. "No one tells Blaze Starr what to do."

Earl had been confined at Mandeville for almost a week, and the only thing I knew about the situation was what I read in the magazines and newspapers and what I heard on television. They described his condition as being very grave. One big-name psychiatrist even described him as being paranoid schizophrenic. I didn't know what the words meant, but that evening I looked it up in the medical dictionary, and I knew then that the doctor didn't know what he was talking about. I wanted to call the doctor and tell him that Earl's fears were not imagined but real.

The following evening during one of my performances at the Sho-Bar, José ran up and motioned for me, interrupting my act. "Governor Earl is on the phone for you," he whispered.

My first reaction was, "He's out!" I rushed to the phone. "Hi there, this is Blaze," I said.

His first words were, "Are you still going to marry me?"

"You bet your bottom dollar I am, more than ever now. Where you at?"

"I'm still down here in Mandeville in the crazy house. It's just like I told you, Blaze. I knew they were going to do this to me. But don't you fret. I'm going to be out of here in a few days, and I'm going to fire every son of a bitch that had anything to do with it. And I'm going to divorce Miz Blanche, and we're going to get married, and

I'm going to make you the First Lady of the great state of Louisiana.''

He sounded as though he was in good spirits, and I asked, ''How are they treating you?''

''Oh, my treatment is all right. But this place is one hell of a mess. It has given me a chance to see firsthand what kind of a condition the mental institutions are in here in this state, and you'd better believe I'm going to do something about it just as soon as I get out of here. I had a heck of a time bribing one of the employees here to let me make a phone call, but I've been using the phone quite frequently today. And I ought to be out of here in just a few days.

''Blaze, there was one of the funniest things happened to me today. I accidentally bumped into one of the nigger patients here. He was a great big man. Actually he bumped into me, and I guess I was feeling a little bad, so I told him to watch where he was going, and then he said something smart back to me. So I said, 'You'd better not talk to me that way, boy, I'm Earl K. Long, governor of the state of Louisiana.' Well, he just glared right back at me and said, 'Oh, you'll be all right in a few days, Mr. Long. When I first came in here, I thought I was Dwight Eisenhower.' I couldn't help laughing.

''I understand the papers and the television people are really making a mess out of me right now. How are they treating you?''

I replied, ''Well, several of them have been after me, but I've managed to escape so far.''

''That's great. You keep up the good work. And you don't say a word to them, you understand?''

''Don't worry about me saying anything,'' I answered. ''Miz Blanche is doing enough talking.''

We talked for thirty or forty minutes, and I was quite relieved to know that Earl was all right. He explained to me that he was physically run down from all the running about that he had been forced to do. But other than that, he said, he was in fairly good shape, considering the fact that the doctors in Texas had made him take pills by the papercupful.

Earl continued to call me from Mandeville every opportunity he had, and I knew it was just a matter of a few days before he would be Louisiana's governor again, just as he had assured me on the telephone. He moved immediately to fire all the top employees of the state mental institution, and he replaced the head man with a friend of his who promptly released him. He also filed for a legal separation from Miz Blanche.

Shortly after Earl's release from Mandeville, I met him at the Roosevelt Hotel. His voice was raspy, he had lost several pounds, and he looked very tired. As I entered his suite, he rose from his chair and walked over and embraced me. "My fair lady," he said, ceremoniously, "let me introduce myself. I am now 'Old Crazy Earl,' governor of the state of Louisiana."

"They have treated you horribly."

As he sat back down, he said, "Yes, I've been through one hell of a mess the last few days. But there's going to be some people to pay for it. I'm not going to rest until I get every damn one of them. Of course, these newspaper reporters are aggravating the hell out of me now. As you noticed when you came in, there must be a hundred of them down there in the lobby. Everywhere I go and everything I say, they're distorting it. If I ain't crazy now, they're going to drive me crazy. I've decided I'm going to take me a vacation. I'm going to go out West, and I want you to go with me."

"Earl, that would be the worst thing in the world, for you and me, if I immediately went off somewhere with you. I think the vacation idea is great, but I think you probably should go alone. That's all the newspapers need to get hold of right now—Blaze Starr and Governor Earl

Long going on vacation together! They would swear you are crazy for sure.''

"Well, I guess you've got a point there. But I tell you one thing, I've got to get out of this state and away from those damn reporters. I figure it'll give me a chance to get rested up here before we get involved in this campaign that's coming up.''

For the most part, Earl was in good spirits in spite of the fact that he was run down physically. He called me every day while he was on his Western vacation. He called me once from Texas and told me that he was going to address the Texas Legislature on the problems of an old man taking on a young wife. I kidded him and told him that topic made about as much sense as anything else, but that he might not have as many problems as he thought.

Regardless of where he was, Earl continued to complain to me about all the newspaper reporters who followed his every footstep. He had thought he would be able to escape them, but somehow or another, they always seemed to know just where he was going to be. He was especially disturbed with some stories that had appeared in *Life* magazine and in *Time*. The *Life* story had a picture of me dancing in a negligee, and at the beginning of the story it had a picture of Earl sitting on a motel bed holding a news conference without his false teeth. Before Mandeville, that kind of picture would have been ignored by the press, but now they were playing up every little angle to make it appear that Earl had actually gone crazy. He told me that as soon as he got back he was going to file a libel suit against the magazine.

One of the things Earl enjoyed most of all was going to the race track and betting on the horses. He had done this for years unnoticed by most. Now each time he went to one of the Western race tracks, the press made big news of it, as if the man were totally insane just because he placed bets on horses. They claimed he was gambling away thousands of dollars.

Other news stories claimed that he was running rampant in the show places of Mexico. Earl loved night life, and prior to the time he was admitted to Mandeville, it was an accepted thing on Bourbon Street to see Governor Long frequenting the night clubs. How strange it was, I thought to myself. Once a man is committed to a mental institution, everything he does takes on new meaning and is considered crazy. People begin to look for all the odd little habits a man might have.

One of the things Earl had always enjoyed doing was going to a store and buying several of the same items. On one occasion, he had bought me twelve hats at the same store. Now, after Mandeville, if he stopped by a store and bought a large quantity of the same item, the press called him crazy. One fact for sure, if Earl Long was crazy when he was in Mandeville and after he came out of Mandeville, then he had been crazy all his life, at least during the time I had known him.

By the time Earl came back to Louisiana, things had begun to calm down somewhat. Miz Blanche had moved out of the mansion and into the recently built house on Millionaire's Road. Earl brought part of his clothing to my apartment, and we lived there together like man and wife. I accepted a few short-run engagements out of town, to places like Las Vegas and Miami, but mostly I worked at the Sho-Bar. Earl didn't like me to go away, and on his account I turned down quite a few big offers.

After talking to me a lot about it, Earl made the decision not to resign as governor and seek re-election. Instead, he selected a long-time buddy, a man by the name of Jimmy Noe, to run as governor, and he planned to run for lieutenant governor. He immediately began making campaign trips throughout the state. Everywhere he went, people flocked out just to get a look at him. He would kid with the audiences and ask them to view for themselves whether he was actually crazy. People loved him. But the newspapers and his one-time political allies who had deserted his ranks once he had been confined had caused enough doubt in people's minds that they were not sure whether he had actually been insane or not. And when the election was finally over in December, Earl and Noe had finished near the bottom in a five-man race. Needless to say, Earl was very disappointed, but he had known for some time prior to the date of the election that he and Noe would be soundly defeated. In the runoff election, Earl threw his support to Jimmie Davis, a former governor of Louisiana, who won handily over DeLesseps Morrison, the Mayor of New Orleans.

Once the election was over, Earl and I lived a quieter life. He would come and go at the apartment, sometimes stopping to bring home an armful of groceries, and I would prepare his favorite dishes. We had dinner at my apartment quite frequently. It was one of the things he liked best to do.

Although he didn't let on much, Earl was quite disturbed that people thought he was crazy. It riled him so that sometimes it just erupted. On one occasion when we were out having dinner at one of his favorite seafood places, he had the waiter bring an extra glass of water to the table, whereupon he astonished everyone in the restaurant by taking out his false teeth and placing them in the water to soak. He looked across the table at me, winked, and whispered, "Just watch them now. Just watch them look around and look at my teeth in this water, and they'll say, 'There's old crazy Earl.' "

Sure enough, everyone who came in and sat down looked around at the teeth and sort of smirked. You didn't need to hear the gossip going on in the restaurant to know that they were all talking about Earl.

A few minutes after putting his teeth in the water, Earl asked the waiter to bring him a paper "poke" and looked over at me with a mischievous grin and said, "I'm really going to give them something to talk about now."

The waiter brought the paper sack, and Earl carefully tore out little holes for his eyes, a hole for his nose, and a hole for his mouth. Then he rolled the paper sack up so it would fit over his head. I couldn't believe it myself, but he pulled the paper sack over his head and sat there for two hours eating shrimp creole and drinking white wine. We snickered back and forth across the table. Everyone in the restaurant thought he was doing it because he was crazy, but I knew he was doing it just for the hell of it, to get a reaction from the crowd.

On our way back to the Sho-Bar that evening, Earl ordered the chauffeur to get over onto the median and drive on the grass. At first, the chauffeur refused, but Earl insisted, so the driver pulled the big limousine over, and away we went at fifty miles an hour. We drove for miles that way, and Earl's comment was, "Well, they claim old Earl is crazy, now for sure they're going to know he's crazy."

Earl was constantly wanting reassurance that I was going to marry him. Every day or two, he would ask, "Are you still going to marry me? You know I've failed to make you the First Lady of Louisiana."

I assured him that being governor of the state was not my reason for marrying him, that I would marry him as soon as his divorce became final. He wanted me to quit stripping, but I explained that stripping was my life, and I loved it as much as he loved politics. I chided him by saying, "If you'll give up politics, I'll give up stripping."

He grinned and said, "Well, I guess I understand how you feel."

I did agree that after we were married, I would strip only about three months out of the year. It was his idea that we would go to Vegas, and I would be booked there. He told me that he would be my "suitcase boy," so that people could call him a gigolo and a pimp.

During this time, we went a lot to the race tracks. Sometimes, Earl would bet a hundred dollars on every horse, thinking I would not know the difference. He would put the tickets in different pockets, remembering which one held the winning ticket. At the end of the race, he would pull out the winning ticket, hand it to me, and say, "Look! You've won! You've won!" I played along with his game and would take the ticket to the window and collect the money.

He was a fanatic over racehorses. One Saturday afternoon, he took me over to the D. J. Stables near New Orleans just to look at the horses. As it turned out, we arrived just in time to witness the birth of a young colt. Earl gazed in absolute amazement as the veterinarian gave a final tug that freed the struggling colt.

Suddenly, he looked at me and said, "That's the most beautiful thing in the world, giving life. And you know, that's the thing I've failed in. Blaze, I want you to have my son. A son to carry on the Long name after I am dead and gone." He reached over and put both arms around me and pulled me close to him.

"I will have your son, Earl. Just as soon as we're married," I said, looking up at him.

He kissed me in full view of everyone. He had said to me several times before that he wanted me to have his son, and I knew this was one of the things that bothered him most. He often talked about how he and Miz Blanche had never been successful in having a baby.

Just as Earl turned back to look at the colt, the owner

of the stables walked over to where we were standing. It was obvious that he and Earl were close friends by the way they greeted one another.

Earl said, "That's sure a beautiful colt. Have you named him yet?"

"No, I don't guess we have." Not sure of himself, he yelled over to a man standing next to the veterinarian. "Have we named the colt yet, L. B.?"

"No," the man answered as he watched the veterinarian busily at work.

"In that case I've got a name for you. Blaze Starr," Earl was fast to say.

The owner looked at me and grinned. "But it's a male."

"I don't give a damn. I want it named Blaze Starr."

"Okay, it's name is Blaze Starr."

Earl looked at me and grinned. "Yes, sir, that colt will be a good one when he grows up. Just mark my words, you'll be reading about that horse."

We all laughed, and I didn't think much more about it until two years later when a friend of mine sent me a newspaper clipping from a New Orleans paper. The heading read, "Blaze Starr Wins Fourth Straight Race," and the Associate Press article reported that "Undefeated Blaze Starr found a hole on the rail at the head of the stretch and with a burst of speed shot through to grab the lead and win the $100,000 Sugar Bowl Handicap at the Fair Grounds today."

Everything was going fine between Earl and me until one of the girls at the Sho-Bar told Earl that I was having an affair with José. José and I had been close friends from the day I started working for him, and since I couldn't drive an automobile, he was constantly taking me places and helping me run errands. I was not aware that Earl was jealous of José until he came into the Sho-Bar late one

154

night. It was around 4 A.M., and there weren't too many people around, probably not more than fifty or sixty customers at the time. I had stayed over at the Sho-Bar later than usual and was sitting at a table with José and two other girls, just sitting there and chatting back and forth, when Earl walked in. He walked up to José, pulled out a .38 special, and held the cold barrel up against José's head.

"You goddamn Mexican," he said, "why don't you go back to Mexico? What the hell are you doing trying to steal my little woman? I am going to blow your goddamn brains out right here and now!"

I was totally shocked by Earl's actions. José turned white in spite of his dark complexion. "What are you talking about, Earl?" he asked.

"You know what I'm talking about. You've been trying to steal my woman."

I chimed in, "That isn't true, Earl."

"Shut up. I know all about it. The son of a bitch has been trying to steal my woman, and he's not going to get away with it."

I said again, "It's just absolutely not so." I kept talking to Earl, trying to persuade him to put the pistol away. I told him that if the press were to come in and see him holding a pistol to a man's head, they would swear for sure that he was crazy. I assured him that I loved him, that I was going to marry him, and that he didn't have to carry on like a sixteen-year-old boy. I said, "If you've got to shoot something, why don't you shoot the stage lights?"

Earl looked at me, then looked at José, and hesitated. Finally, he said, "All right, we'll have a shootout. We'll stand back here, and we'll shoot at the stage lights. And if you're a better shot than I am, José, you can have my little woman."

José agreed, and they walked back midways in the Sho-

Bar. By this time, most of the customers had realized what was happening and had fled the building. The band quit playing and ran for their lives.

Earl raised the pistol and carefully aimed at one of the lantern lights that hung above the stage. He pulled the trigger, there was a loud explosion, and the lantern shattered. He handed the gun to José and said, "Here, you little son of a bitch, let's see if you can shoot."

José, trembling somewhat from his experience, held the gun up and shot. Like Earl, he was on target. A lantern exploded, and glass flew in every direction.

On the second shot, Earl missed. José took the gun again, aimed, and shot. He hit, then carefully unloaded the gun and handed it back to Earl. "Now to prove to you that I'm not having an affair with your little lady, I'm going to give her to you right now."

Earl acted a little sheepish, then both of them broke into a roar of laughter and slapped each other on the back. Earl grabbed me by the arm and led me outside to the waiting limousine, and off we went to the mansion. Luckily, the press was nowhere around to record the incident. Earl admitted that it was a stupid thing he had done and promised he would never make such a public display again.

Two weeks later, it was my turn to get jealous. Earl had slipped off and gone to New York without telling me a thing about it. He was gone for almost a week. When he did come back, he came into the Sho-Bar carrying several huge boxes and asked for me. I thought to myself, "If Earl has a right to get jealous, I think I'll use this occasion to show him that I have a right to get jealous, too." I walked back to Earl's table and said, "Just where in the hell have you been?"

He grinned from ear to ear. "I've been to New York," he said. "You can just call me the big fur man from up North."

"Yeah, I know, you've been up there messing around with some of those other women."

He hastily opened the box and held up a fur. It was a white mink. He handed it to me. "Here, I've got you a mink for every day of the week. I want to make up with my baby."

I grabbed the white mink, threw it in the floor, and jumped up and down on it. "I'm not interested in your minks. Besides, the weather is too warm to wear them down here anyway."

Earl stood, shocked, and the expression on his face was one of sheer amazement at my antics.

I continued to jump up and down on the white mink. I yelled, "It's my turn to be crazy. If you can get yourself photographed wearing a pillowcase over your head or your false teeth sitting in a glass of water, I can get photographed jumping up and down on one of your goddamn white minks!"

When I said that, he roared with laughter, and, looking around at the bystanders, he said, "She loves me! She loves me!"

I realized then that Earl was rubbing off on me. My mother always told me that if you stay around someone long enough, you get so you look and act just like him. I grabbed Earl and kissed him. Then I took the white mink to my dressing room where I would have it available to use in my act. The other six we loaded into the limousine and took to my apartment.

About a week later, Earl accused me once again of having an affair with José. This time I became very angry and left Earl at the apartment by himself. Later that night I received a call at the Sho-Bar from Earl's bodyguard, and he told me that Earl wanted me to know that he was at the 500 Club with Tee Tee Red, a stripper.

I was mad as a wet hen, and as I hung up the phone I

yelled to José, "I'm going down to the 500 Club to beat the hell out of the governor."

"What are you talking about?" he asked, astonished.

"That's right, I'm going down and beat the hell right out of him. He's down there with that stripper, Tee Tee Red!"

"You can't do that, you'll be arrested."

"Oh, yeah? Well, you just come and watch."

Several people heard me and knew what I was up to, and by the time I walked to the 500 Club, there must have been forty to fifty people following along behind me. When I arrived at the club, Earl was sitting at a table with Tee Tee. I walked up and slapped him with my open hand, right in the face. He grabbed his heart and pretended that I had really hurt him. But I knew he was faking it, and I continued my rampage, kicking over chairs and finally turning over the table where they sat. Tee Tee ran to her dressing room.

Earl jumped to his feet and asked, "What the hell have I ever done to you?"

"You're with another woman," I said as I slapped him three or four more times. I then ran as hard as I could back to the Sho-Bar and hid, for I figured I would be arrested.

A few minutes later, Earl arrived, wiping his face with one hand and holding his jaw with the other. "Give me some ice. She's just about killed me," he said to one of the bartenders. "Where is she?" he asked as the bartender handed him a towel with some ice cubes wrapped inside.

I was close enough to overhear everything, and, sensing that he was not too angry, I came out of my hiding place. When he saw me, he started laughing. "Come on, I'm not mad. That was nothing. Just a love pat. That means you love me," he said as he embraced me and kissed me in front of everyone.

One night around this time, or maybe it was a little later in the year—I don't remember exactly—Earl brought Senator and Mrs. Jack Kennedy to the Sho-Bar. He was always bringing visitors in to see my act. We all sat at Earl's table and talked, and afterwards he told me, "That young man is going to be president some day, Blaze, mark my words." I couldn't believe it. Jack seemed like too much of a kid even to be a senator. He was nice, and so was Jackie, though she didn't have much to say.

Earl's term as governor had almost expired when he came into the Sho-Bar one evening and told me that we were going to have one big last fling at the mansion. He wanted me to invite all the girls at the Sho-Bar over to the mansion after we got off work that evening. So I spread the word around to all the girls, and they all thought it was a great way to spend the evening. Altogether there were eight or ten of us who piled into Earl's limousine around one o'clock in the morning and headed towards Baton Rouge and the mansion. We sang and joked all the way, and I sat partially in Earl's lap until he complained about getting tired. Then I moved to the bottom, and I held him. He had gained back some of the weight he had lost and was a rather hefty load. I must admit that my legs were a little tired by the time we arrived at the mansion in Baton Rouge.

Earl rang the doorbell, and a sleepy-eyed butler opened the front door. Earl called him by his first name and said, "You can go on home now. Me and the girls are going to have us a little party."

We all went into the ballroom of the mansion, and Earl began setting out bottles of champagne, along with some Scotch and bourbon. For this occasion, he said, he was going to break over and have a little sip of bourbon. He opened up a Coke, poured half of it out, filled the rest of the bottle with bourbon, and began sipping. I stayed with the champagne.

We were all in a good mood, singing, joking, and laughing and carrying on. Earl was reminiscing about all his accomplishments as governor of the state. He talked some about his brother Huey and made a toast to his nephew, Senator Russell, and his wife, Blanche, and said, "May their souls rest in hell!" as he reminded us that this was the very room where they had met and decided to send him to the mental institution in Texas.

We all held up our glasses, and all the girls chimed in and said, "May their souls rest in hell!"

Earl finished drinking his drink from the Coke bottle and flung the bottle against the chandelier at the far end of the room. Glass flew in every direction. All the girls turned up their drinks, finished them, and threw their glasses at the chandelier.

Earl yelled out, "How about a last strip in the governor's mansion, Blaze?"

All the girls started clapping their hands. I jumped up on the table and said, "I've got to have some music if I'm going to strip."

Earl rushed out of the room and was gone for three or four minutes. He came back with a radio, plugged it in, and turned it on to one of the local stations that was playing a song by Elvis Presley. I began to move back and forth on the table. Earl sat down at the other end, all rared back as if he were sitting at the stage of the Sho-Bar. I began casually taking off all my clothes. All the other girls were standing around the table, clapping their hands and yelling, "Take it off! Take it off!" Elvis was yelling, "You ain't nothing but a hound dog . . ."

The song ended, but I continued dancing until the next one came on. It was a little different beat, but it didn't interrupt my dancing. I threw clothes in every direction until I stood there, stripped to my panties, dancing the last dance in the mansion for Earl. Two or three of the other girls started dancing and stripping, and within the next ten minutes, they had all stripped down to their panties. Earl loved every minute of it, and at the end, he held his Coke bottle up and said, "Here's to the strippers! Here's to the state of Louisiana! Here's to Earl Long! May he live forever!"

It must have taken fifteen or twenty minutes to separate our clothes and get dressed again. It was almost daylight when Earl suggested that we probably should get some boxes and start crating up all his belongings. We spent the next two hours crating all the silver, the china, and practically everything else that was not fastened to the walls. We carted them downstairs and loaded them into the limousine and every other available vehicle. Later in the morning, a four-car caravan led by the governor's limousine made its way from Baton Rouge back to my apartment in New Orleans where we unloaded all the mansion booty.

We never stayed at the mansion after that. Earl's term expired with him living with me in my apartment in New Orleans.

On the day of the inauguration of Governor-elect Jimmy Davis, Earl Long and I rode in the parade through the streets of Baton Rouge in an open convertible. Earl had a whole box of pictures of himself with the inscription, "I'd like to be a friend of everybody. Yours forever, Earl K. Long." He was in a good mood, and you would have thought that it was he who would shortly be sworn in as governor.

I wore what Earl referred to as my "schoolteaching outfit," a two-piece white suit and a striped blouse that was fastened with a bow at the neck. Earl had bought me a white net hat especially for the inaugural two days before. I looked just about as respectable as any of the other ladies in the crowd of dignitaries.

Earl took my hand and led me through the crowd to the inaugural platform. Occasionally, he would stop and chat momentarily with a friend. One man he was talking to offered Earl a cigarette. Earl took it, grinning broadly, and said, "Thanks, I'll smoke anything as long as it's not a Picayune." Everybody laughed at the outgoing governor's final jibe at the New Orleans newspaper that was probably his worst political enemy.

There were more television cameras and newspaper reporters paying attention to Earl and me than to the swearing-in of the new governor. We were having a great time. I had never seen Earl so relaxed. When he wasn't leaning over the platform rail talking with someone, he was taking pictures of me with his movie camera, and I, in turn, took pictures of him.

Earl had his pockets stuffed with handkerchiefs. He first pulled out a big red bandanna and wiped perspiration from his forehead. When that one was damp, he took a blue one of the same size and style from his hip pocket and continued the process. Earl finally pulled a white handkerchief from his pocket, combined it with the blue and red ones, and began waving them briskly to the crowd amidst a roar of laughter and applause. He glanced over at Governor Davis and said, "I'm probably worth more going out than you are going in."

Davis did not respond, but a time or two he glanced our way and seemed a little perturbed that Earl was getting so much of the attention.

As we made our way back to the Sho-Bar after all the speeches, Earl whispered to me that he was going to run for Congress.

"You're crazy!" I protested.

"Don't tell me that," he said. "Everybody has told me I'm crazy."

"Well, I didn't mean it that way. But you know you don't have a chance in the world to be elected to Congress.

Why don't you forget politics? Let's get married and forget about all of it.''

"No," he said. "I wasn't able to make you the First Lady of Louisiana, so I'm going to make you the First Lady of the United States. I'm going to run for Congress, then I'm going to run for the presidency. And as soon as I get elected to Congress, we're going to get married.''

It was late in the evening when we continued our discussion of his plans to run for Congress. After my performance at the Sho-Bar, he laid the plan out quickly.

"I know that I can win the election for Congress in my home district. You go on back to Baltimore and dance at the Two O'Clock Club. I'll start telling everybody you went back to West Virginia and married a schoolteacher, and we'll get that part of it out of the news. You go ahead and buy us a house in Baltimore, and I'll commute back and forth from Washington.''

I did as Earl suggested. I went back to Baltimore, looked around, and bought myself a nice, spacious home with a big garden and a swimming pool. I began working once again at the Two O'Clock Club with Mr. Goodman. During the next weeks, Earl called constantly, telling me all about his plans and how the campaign was shaping up. The night before the election, he called me and told me that he was going to win for certain and that just as soon as the election was over, he was going to put on a black wig and a mustache and fly directly to Baltimore, and we would celebrate his victory together.

That was my last conversation with Earl Long. The next day when I attempted to call him, there was no answer. I called several times during the next three or four days, and each time the phone rang, but there was no answer. Earl had suffered a heart attack on the day of the election and evidently refused to seek medical attention for fear that it would leak out and hurt his chances. After winning a smashing victory in the Democratic primary election over incumbent Congressman Herbert B. McSween, which was tantamount to being elected directly to the Congress since the Republican Party never offered any notable opposition in the general election, he died a few days later, a congressman who never made it to D.C.

I caught a plane to New Orleans when I heard of his death. Heartbroken and fighting to hold back the tears as I walked past his casket, I pulled a red rose from where I had it fastened to my bosom and laid it among the funeral wreaths with a silent prayer for "old crazy Earl." I loved the man.

13

Immediately following Earl Long's death, there was a nasty controversy over a will in which he left me fifty thousand dollars. His two sisters were also named to receive a portion of his estate, but Miz Blanche, through legal maneuverings, was able to nullify the will. One of Earl's sisters wrote me a letter asking if I was going to take any action. She said she had a photostatic copy of the original will naming us all as beneficiaries. I told her that I wasn't interested in pursuing the matter, that people would think that I had maintained my relationship with Earl only to get his money. I also told her that "old lady Long" had a greater need for Earl's estate than I did since she had the big mansion to keep up on Millionaire's Road. However, I did urge the sister to get herself a good lawyer and see if she couldn't make a fight for at least a part of the estate. I knew that Earl's sisters were not wealthy and certainly cold use whatever Earl might have decided to leave them.

When newspaper reporters attempted to get me to make

a statement regarding the matter, I refused. I had been terribly saddened and distressed at Earl's death, and talk about his estate and wills continued to upset me. One night when a friend asked me about it, I got angry. "Goddammit," I remember yelling, "I don't want the money. I just *liked* the man. Goddammit, I loved him!"

Unfortunately, Earl had never seen the house that I had purchased in Baltimore, the house in which we were to live after he was elected to Congress and we were married. It was no mansion like the one on Millionaire's Road, but by my standards it was quite an elegant house. It was located on Queen Anne Road on the outskirts of Baltimore on a one-and-one-half-acre wooded lot. The living room alone was larger than the entire cabin that I had been raised in back in Newground Hollow. The six-foot iron picket fence that surrounded the lot and the swimming pool in the rear made it a lovely place. I am sure Earl would have been pleased with it. When I wasn't working at the Two O'Clock Club, I spent hours remodeling and decorating the house. For a long time, I didn't want to go anywhere else.

Finally, I began taking out-of-town engagements again, and so it was that almost a year after Earl's death I found myself booked for six weeks at the Sho-Bar on Bourbon Street. I considered canceling the contract. During the year I had received a number of anonymous phone calls, supposedly from Louisiana, all telling me that I should never return to the state and that I would be killed if I did.

This time when I arrived in New Orleans, there was no limousine waiting to pick me up at the airport. There were no newspapermen or reporters waiting for an interview. I could not help but look around for Ollie Butler or one of Earl's other chauffeurs when I stepped off the plane. But instead of riding to the Sho-Bar in the governor's limousine, I rode a taxi.

Even the Sho-Bar itself was different, and I thought to

myself how strange it was how things could change so drastically in a year's time. It was almost impossible for me to go on stage without looking around the room for Earl or waiting in anticipation of one of his phone calls, beckoning me off into the night on an unpredictable venture. Without Earl, New Orleans certainly was not the same city. In fact, the first week that I performed at the Sho-Bar, I was miserable. I wanted to leave, but José talked me out of it. He kept saying that things would settle down after a few days. Instead, things got worse.

Anonymous telephone calls started pouring into the Sho-Bar, all threatening my life if I didn't leave at once. José attempted to reassure me by telling me that it was probably only some crackpot trying to harass me and that I should ignore the calls altogether. However, they continued to come in on a frequent basis, and at the end of three weeks, I had had all I could take of New Orleans. I canceled my contract and boarded the next flight to Baltimore.

For the most part after that, I worked full time at the Two O'Clock Club, although I occasionally made trips to other cities for as long as two weeks. I was starting to feel pretty good about my life again. For one thing, I was making good money, over fifty grand a year, and for another, the threatening phone calls had subsided, although I still did get them occasionally when I was home in Baltimore. After a while, I was able to rationalize these calls as idle threats—that is, I could until late one night after I came home from the Two O'Clock Club.

I was alone that evening in the huge house. Debbie, my younger sister, who normally lived with me, had gone back to West Virginia for a week's vacation to visit our parents. It was nearing 3 A.M., and being somewhat tired from work, I didn't spend much time getting ready for bed. I had hardly lain down and flipped off the light when all of a sudden a man appeared in the dark room. Standing over me, he pinned me to the bed, holding one hand on my shoulder and the other one around my neck. I did manage to turn on a bed lamp before I was completely overpowered, and as long as I live I shall never forget the expression on his face nor his features in the circle of light from the lamp. He was a young man, probably in his late twenties, with blond hair. He was handsome, and even under those most precarious circumstances, I could not help but notice the unusual blue-gray color of his eyes.

My first reaction was that he had followed me home from the Two O'Clock Club and was going to rape me. I figured that if this were the case, maybe I could talk him out of it. Without showing the fright I felt, I said, "Please, you don't have to hold me by the neck. Let's talk this thing over." There was no immediate reaction from the young man.

"You are hurting me," I pleaded. He eased the pressure on my throat but still held me firmly. It still was somewhat difficult for me to talk. "Please, please, let's talk this thing over," I said again. "You don't have to be violent."

Suddenly, he said, "Look, I am not here to rape you. I am not interested in sleeping with you. I have a job to do. I am being paid for it, and if you cooperate, nothing will happen."

"What do you want?" I asked. "Tell me what you want."

"Okay, I'm going to release you, but if you move, you're in trouble."

I said, "Yes, sir." I had become accustomed to sleeping in the nude, and I gingerly edged the sheet up to cover my bosom. I had a .38 revolver under my mattress. If I could reach it . . . But he had one knee directly over it, and even my pulling up the sheet had earned me another stern order, "Don't move."

He reached into the inner pocket of his coat and pulled

out a piece of paper. "As I told you, Miss Starr," he said in an almost polite, quite formal manner, "I have a job to do, and I have to get it completed 100 per cent before I get paid. I have here before me a list of jewelry that Governor Earl Long gave you. My job is to collect all that jewelry."

"But I don't have any jewelry here," I lied.

He slapped me across the face, not hard, but firmly. "Don't feed me a line of shit, young lady. As a matter of fact, I have already collected all the items with the exception of the five-carat diamond ring and one or two other times. I found them in the box in the back of the linen closet."

I knew then that this was for real, and I also knew that he had found the jewelry as he claimed, for the linen closet was where I kept everything hidden. Altogether, Earl had probably given me eighty to ninety thousand dollars' worth of different types of jewelry. I just had never thought about anybody stealing it or wanting it back, so I hadn't taken any extra precautions with it. I had heard about a lot of people keeping their jewelry in safety deposit boxes and all sorts of odd places, but I had always figured that if I couldn't keep it where I could wear it when I wanted to, then it wasn't any use to me anyway. The five-carat diamond I always kept in a small juice glass in the back of the china cabinet. I very seldom wore it for fear that I might be mugged in the tough streets where I worked on The Block. Not only was the ring the most valuable piece of jewelry that Earl had bought me, but I cherished it more than any of the others.

"All you've got to do, Miss Starr," the young man said, "is give me these other pieces of jewelry, and I'll be on my way, and no one will get hurt."

All those threatening phone calls of the year since Earl's death now flashed through my mind, and I felt sure the young man was going to kill me unless I did as he said.

Maybe even then. But I didn't want to give up Earl's ring without a fight. "If you got the jewelry out of the linen closet, you got it all. That is all that I have here, honest," I pleaded.

"I don't get paid unless I bring it all."

I had on my finger a large diamond ring that a group of club owners had given me as a bonus when I performed in New York years before. It was fairly large, but it was certainly not a five-carat diamond. The young man grabbed my hand and held it up. "There's the ring I want. You're wearing it!"

"No! Earl didn't give me that ring," I said.

"Come on. Pull it off! Pull it off!" he demanded.

"But it won't come off. I have had that ring on for years, and it just won't come off."

He grabbed my hand and tugged at the ring until my finger began to swell, making the ring even more difficult to move back and forth. I pleaded to him that he was hurting me, but he ignored me. "Where's the bathroom?" he demanded.

I said, "Over there."

"Okay, come on. We'll go over and soak it in warm water and see if we can't pull it off that way. Soap and warm water ought to take it off."

"Would you please let me get some clothes on."

"Look baby, I am not interested in your body. All I am interested in is that ring, and let's get it off right now. I don't have time to fool with you." He jerked me out of the bed, and I walked with him, totally nude, to the bathroom. He turned on the hot water and practically scalded my hand, demanding that I rub soap on my finger. I did as he said, but still the ring was firm and would not move.

"Damn you," he said, "I'm going to get that ring one way or another. Where is a knife?"

"You can't cut the ring off with a knife," I said. "There's no way you're going to be able to get it under the ring. Besides, you can't cut it off with a knife, and I don't have a saw or anything in the house.''

''Come on,'' he insisted. ''Let's go to the kitchen. Let's find that knife.''

I had no idea what he had in mind. Needless to say, however, I was concerned that he might cut my finger in his effort to cut off the ring. I continued to plead with him, but it was useless.

As we entered the kitchen, a car pulled up into the driveway and turned its lights off. I thought for a second that maybe someone was coming to the house who could rescue me, but the young man said, ''Don't get excited. It's just my partner. He's waiting for me until I bring the jewelry.''

He took a big butcher knife out of the drawer and walked over to the kitchen sink. He held my hand out and said. ''Turn your head. It won't hurt that much.''

All of a sudden I realized the he intended to cut off my finger. I knew I couldn't let that happen if it was at all possible to prevent it. Realizing that time was running out on me, I twisted away, raised my knee and hit him firmly between the legs. He dropped the knife and bent over, groaning and twisting in pain. He yelled, ''You bitch! You bitch!''

I fled towards the bedroom. Still bent over and holding himself, he staggered towards me. I had dealt him a firm blow, but I had not put him completely out of commission. Just as I managed to pull the revolver from beneath the mattress, he grabbed my wrist and hit me solidly on the chin. The pistol shook loose and went sliding across the room. I tried to fight back, but he soon overpowered me. He pulled a straight razor from his back pocket and began slashing at me. He cut me first on my arm as I raised it to protect my face. Then as I struggled to get free, he cut me across the hip, and finally he slashed me across the breast. I knew then that he intended to kill me. I also knew that I would not be able to stop him. So I decided to just roll over and play dead, hoping that he would not hurt me any more. I fell backwards, hitting very hard on the floor, and lay still.

For a moment there was complete silence. I could feel the blood oozing out of the wounds. I figured he would slice my throat for good measure, and as I lay there bleeding, I began to pray. I heard the car horn blow out on the lawn, and I heard footsteps move towards the bedroom door. After what seemed to be an eternity, I heard the back door close. But I still lay there afraid to move. I didn't try to get up until I heard the car speed from the driveway.

When I opened my eyes, I saw that I was covered in blood, and the room was a shambles. I knew I had only a few minutes before I lost consciousness. I grabbed the telephone and managed to call an ambulance.

Within a short time, I was in a Baltimore hospital. I had lost an enormous amount of blood, but the doctors assured me that I would be all right. I was naturally most concerned about the three-inch gash across my breast. I was afraid my career had been ruined. The doctors told me that skin transplants would hide everything, however, and I had to believe them.

It was late the next day before I could give a detailed report to the police. During the days that followed, it was determined that two men, one answering my description of the blue-eyed blond, had flown from New Orleans to Baltimore and had rented a car the day before the robbery. They had returned the car early the next morning and flown back to New Orleans. Naturally, they had used fictitious names, and the police were never able to trace them.

As soon as the wounds healed, I began a process of skin grafts that was to last for almost two years. In time, all the scars were repaired except the one under my arm, which I chose to ignore. The thieves had managed to take all the major pieces of jewelry Earl had bought for me except the big ring. I guess it was stupid of me not to have told the man with the strange blue eyes where the ring was, but everything happened so suddenly, I hardly had time to think. I just reacted. To avoid any future break-ins, I purchased a German police dog, which was fully trained to handle intruders. And within three weeks of the attack, with plenty of makeup to hide my still-fresh scars, I was back on stage at the Two O'Clock Club.

14

Working at the Two O'Clock Club every night and living in Baltimore became a routine to which I had difficulty adjusting, and once my first round of skin grafts was finished, I arranged with Mr. Goodman to go on the road again. I would generally work three weeks on the road and one week at the Two O'Clock Club each month. I continued with this work schedule through the mid-1960s. Then I decided to settle permanently in Baltimore and strip solely at the Two O'Clock Club. I suppose I had got my fill of traveling around the country.

Besides, stripping, exotic dancing, and burlesque in general began a decline in the mid-1960s as a result of the new permissive attitude towards sex and nudity that was developing in the United States. A man didn't have to go to a strip club or a burlesque theater to see a pair of tits. He could go to one of the new restaurants opening all over the place and feast his eyes on a topless waitress while he ate his lunch or dinner. Then came the X-rated movies, and in many cities the next step was that exotic dancing turned into displays of total nudity as many once-respected strip clubs had their girls throw away their G-strings in order to keep up. Like the steam locomotive trying to compete with the new diesel trains, there was no doubt that burlesque was giving way to total nudity. But just as there were those who would walk ten miles to view a steam locomotive or even pay two dollars to make a two-mile trip on it, there were those who would still patronize traditional burlesque shows and places like the Two O'Clock Club that feature old-style stripping. So, despite the fact that I was, on numerous occasions, offered very lucrative contracts to perform in the nudie clubs, I declined and decided to ride out the storm on The Block.

During the five or six years after Earl Long's death, I had not dated any other men seriously until I met Jimmy Stern—a man a few years younger than I, personable and intelligent, who worked as a bartender in one of the many clubs on The Block and was terribly ambitious to become a club owner himself.

After a few months, Jimmy moved in with me in my house on Queen Anne Road. We figured it made more sense to live together for a while to determine if we really loved each other, and to see how things would work out between us. If after a year or two everything worked out all right, we agreed, we would talk seriously about marriage. To me the arrangement was excellent. Jimmy and I were constant companions, yet we both continued to be rather independent individuals. I could come and go as I pleased, and he did the same. It was a beautiful relationship. There were no quarrels or arguments. I began to think that legalizing an affair was what broke up many couples and wondered if Carroll and I had never married whether we might still have been friends living together.

I didn't dare write and tell my mother that I had a man in the house for fear that she would totally misunderstand. Marriage had always been a sacred institution to her, mainly because she and my father had always been so happy together. So I kept everything a big secret where she was concerned.

Jimmy had been living at my house for almost two years when he came in one evening terribly excited and told me about a bar on The Block that was up for sale. The price was thirty thousand dollars. Inside an hour, he had convinced me that it was a great opportunity for the two of us and wanted to know if I could raise that much money. I told him I could.

During the years, I had managed to make some fairly decent investments as a result of having an excellent business adviser as well as friend in Mr. Goodman. Generally, I would discuss all my financial affairs with him before making a final decision. This time, however, I secretly cashed in several stocks and bonds without consulting him. Within a week, Jimmy owned his own little bar. He agreed to pay me back at the rate of two hundred dollars a month. But since we were living together, and very happily, I really wasn't concerned about repayment. I figured that we would eventually get married and that would settle it all up, anyway.

I had bought Jimmy a new lavender Cadillac for his birthday three months before, and when some of my close friends found out what I had done now, they told me that I was crazier than hell. I tried to explain to them that Jimmy and I were deeply in love and that he was one of the most considerate and trustworthy persons that I had ever met. When he was not working at the bar, he devoted every free minute he had to me.

As time passed, however, I began to get somewhat curious about Jimmy's behavior in some regards. For one thing, he didn't want me to patronize his club. He claimed that when he was at work, all of his time should be devoted to the operation of the bar. If I was there, he said, it would distract him. I thought that made sense, so normally I stayed away. But one afternoon when I stopped by for a few minutes, a young woman came in and, in my presence, handed him a ring and kissed him on the cheek. It was a small ring, which he placed on his little finger. Then he looked around at me, grinned sheepishly, and introduced me to the young woman, whose name was Mike Shultz. I hardly knew what to say. I figured it was some kind of joke. But then Jimmy explained that Mike was a female impersonator who worked at one of the clubs on The Block.

I laughed it all off, but during the next few days Jimmy continued to wear the ring, and this puzzled me enough that finally I brought the subject up and asked him how come. He was incensed, quite unlike his usual pleasant self, and snapped at me, "Christ, if you're that interested in the ring, I'll give it to you." I told him that I wasn't interested in it at all but was curious about why he would wear a ring given to him by a man.

I became more concerned about our relationship when Jimmy started leaving the house regularly every Sunday afternoon around two o'clock and not returning until sometimes eight or ten that evening, never offering any explanation as to where he was going or telling me when he got in where he had been. It was not that I really questioned his whereabouts. We had an understanding, and I enjoyed our independence as much as he did. But out of courtesy, I would always tell him when I was going out, where I was going, and with whom I would be. Until recently, he had always done the same thing, and it was this change, his failure to tell me anything about his plans, that began to worry me.

The more I thought about it, the more I was convinced that he had met another woman. And after several weekends of the unexplained Sunday departures, I finally did a terrible thing. I engaged a private detective agency in Baltimore to follow him. The next morning, the detective reported that he had followed Jimmy to an apartment building, that he had entered at approximately 3 P.M., and had remained there until seven that evening. There was no longer any doubt in my mind that there was another woman.

I felt guilty, however, about having Jimmy followed and told myself that I would never do a thing like that again. I didn't mention to him that I was suspicious, or perhaps jealous. And for the most part our relationship continued to be very beautiful—except on Sunday afternoons. Week after week, he would leave after lunch and be gone for five, six, sometimes as much as eight hours every Sunday.

Finally it got the best of me, and I had to know. I called the detective agency once again and asked them to see if they could find out for certain where Jimmy was going and what he was doing with his Sundays.

Jimmy didn't come home at all the Sunday after I had called the detective the second time, and it was early the next morning before I was able to reach the man to find out what had happened. He reported that he had followed Jimmy to the same apartment and this time posed as a repairman for the apartment building. When he knocked on the door, a young man answered and invited him in. Inside was Jimmy, totally nude and wearing a red wig. There were also three other males, all nude and made up like women. The detective added that he was sure they would never have answered the door except that they were obviously high on some drug.

When I had heard the entire story, I was unable to speak. I was sick all over. It crossed my mind that maybe the wig was mine, one of the ones I sometimes wore in the club when I didn't have time to go through the three-hour business of getting my own heavy head of hair done. I ran to the closet where I kept my wigs and checked. I was right. One of them was missing. A depression like I had never experienced before came over me, and for the next few days I refused to go to work or to talk to anyone, even on the telephone. It was bad enough to have lost my husband, Carroll, to another woman, but even worse to lose Jimmy to another man. I thought there must be something wrong with me. I began to question my ability to satisfy a man, to make any man happy. And the more I attempted to unravel what had happened, the more confused I became.

It was three weeks before Jimmy finally came home. I tried to pretend that I didn't know what had happened. But it was hopeless. I couldn't. Jimmy, too, tried to pretend that nothing had happened and to act like he had only been gone for a few hours. It was silly, especially since it was evident from his extreme nervousness that he was aware that I knew more than I was letting on.

Finally, my temper and my hurt feelings got the best of me, and I asked angrily, "Where in hell have you been?"

He attempted to apologize for not letting me know where he was. But without giving me any real explanation, he simply said that he would not let it happen again.

"Why didn't you tell me you had problems?" I asked.

"What are you talking about?"

"You know damn well what I'm talking about. If you had told me from the beginning, perhaps I could have accepted it. Now I find it very difficult to understand, or to know what to do about it."

"What are you talking about?" he asked again.

"Damn it! You know what I'm talking about. You like men, not women. You used me. You simply used me to get yourself a lavender Cadillac and the money to buy your club."

He looked at me and began to cry. "Then you do know. You do know that I have a problem. I can't help it. Believe me, Blaze, I love you, but I just can't help it. I have tried every way in the world to fight it, but I just can't. I can't.

"How can you love me and do me this way?"

He sat down on the couch, still crying and sobbing like a little baby. I could not help but feel sorry for him, for I believed that he was telling me the truth about his situation.

Finally, he looked up and said, "Can I come back? Can I come back and live with you in the house and let's let things go on as they were before and give me another chance?"

"I'm sorry," I replied. "I just couldn't. You've destroyed our relationship. You've destroyed me mentally. I could never sleep with you again. I'm sorry, but how could I live with you, knowing that you're in love with a man?"

"Blaze, if you'll take me back, I'll go see a psychiatrist and see if I can get this problem straightened out."

"Well, I think that's what you probably should do. You should go see a psychiatrist. Maybe I should, too. You've made me think there's something wrong with me. But I don't believe I could ever get over the fact that you don't really love me. I just don't think I can handle the situation. I'm sorry."

I had placed all of Jimmy's clothing out in the living room with the expectation that eventually he would come back to the house to retrieve his belongings. I told him what I had done and suggested that he pack and leave as quickly as possible. I also told him that I expected him to repay what he still owed me on the thirty thousand dollars for the bar immediately. In full.

After he left, I was even more confused and unhappy than I had been the three weeks he was gone. It took me several more weeks to get myself in shape to go back to work. Finally, I had to sit down with Mr. Goodman and tell him what had happened. He was concerned that I hadn't explained to him earlier about lending Jimmy the money to buy the bar, but he assured me that everything would work out in the end and attempted to console me as best he could.

From the very beginning of our association, I had always felt reassured when I talked with Mr. Goodman. He was such a steady and level-headed gentleman and always very kind to me. This time was no exception. He was calm, his usual self, but near the end of our conversation, he surprised me by asking whether, since I was apparently in the mood to buy bars, I would like to purchase the Two O'Clock Club. "You're not serious, are you?" I asked. "You wouldn't give up the Two O'Clock Club after all these years."

"Yes, to tell you the truth, Blaze, I would like to give it up. I suppose I am very attached to it, but things are getting so I really need to devote all my time to my theatrical agency. And you're about the only person in the world that I know of that I would sell the Two O'Clock Club to. You know, you've helped make it what it is. You could advertise it as your own club and be the featured star every night."

There was no need to spend several days pondering the situation. I knew that Mr. Goodman had been disturbed by rumors that a race riot on The Block was imminent. There was ample reason for concern. There had been riots not long before in Washington and Detroit, and Baltimore was no different for the blacks—maybe worse. Basically, Mr. Goodman was also worried about what was happening to show business and generally just disgusted with what was happening in America. I didn't really share his fears, though maybe I should have, and on the spot I took him up on his offer. Two weeks later, I was the proud owner of the Two O'Clock Club.

The employees could hardly believe that I was the new boss, and, needless to say, I was terribly excited with my new role. I was determined to work around the clock to make the club a success, and during the next two or three months, I did work almost twenty-four hours a day, learning all I could about the management end of it. I had never before realized all the many problems that could come up in operating a business. Purchasing the whiskey, paying the bills, keeping the time for the bartenders, the waiters and waitresses, and the strippers, writing the paychecks, and above all listening to all the personal problems of my employees—it was a time-consuming job. In the past, these were the problems that Mr. and Mrs. Goodman had devoted their attention to, and until now I had never realized just how much time it took. But I enjoyed every minute of it and made money right from the beginning. The hard work of running the Two O'Clock Club on my own was also helping me to forget Jimmy and my own severe psychological problems that had developed as a result of my relationship with him. I had more or less convinced myself I'd gotten over him, if not the aftereffects of my disillusionment—until one evening when I was going to work and saw Jimmy and a young girl drive up in front of his club and park the Cadillac I had bought him.

On impulse, I immediately walked across the street and struck the girl across the face with my fist. The edge of my diamond cut into her eyebrow, and blood ran down the side of her face. I was back in the Two O'Clock Club before I fully realized what I had done. This incident only tended to confuse me more about myself. I knew that I shouldn't have vented my anger against Jimmy or the girl, and why I hit her, I shall never know. I felt terrible about it.

A week later, Jimmy called me and told me that he and the girl intended to sue me for ten thousand dollars. They were at Jimmy's club with their attorney, and he said they would like to have a meeting with me. He added that it could be very injurious to me if I had to go to court. As the new owner of the Two O'Clock Club, it would certainly make me look bad, and he would see to it that the newspapers carried the story. It would be simpler, he said, if I just went ahead and paid the ten thousand dollars.

I was speechless when I heard what he said. Restraining myself as much as possible, I told Jimmy that maybe he and the girl and their attorney could come over to the Two O'Clock Club where we could talk about it. He said that they would be right over.

Sitting there waiting for them to come in, I became so angry that I actually began to shake all over. To think that Jimmy would attempt to blackmail me—when he still owed me more than twenty-eight thousand dollars for the bar. And the lavender Cadillac that he was riding around in had not cost him one cent!

It was midafternoon, and there was no one at the club but me. I had come down to straighten up the place in preparation for that night's business. Within a few minutes, Jimmy, his girl friend, and the attorney arrived. Just seeing Jimmy and the girl revived all my hostility and on impulse I hit the girl again, knocking her to the floor. Then I grabbed a beer bottle and struck Jimmy a glancing blow as he ran from the club. The girl quickly scrambled to her feet and ran after him. The lawyer had already left.

I laughed out loud. That was what they did back in West Virginia on Saturday nights at the beer taverns. Two men would square off with each other, and each one would grab a beer bottle. Whoever got the first lick in usually won the fight. The doctors were always busy on Sunday morning sewing up the wounds.

Shortly after that incident, Jimmy sold his bar to another man, and I was able to collect the balance of the money he owed me. There was never any further mention of the suit he and the girl had threatened me with for hitting her the first time. But if I was out of the woods financially as far as Jimmy was concerned, emotionally I certainly wasn't. My experience with him had done something to me. I found myself turned against all men in general. I occasionally went out, mainly to see if I could regain some perspective. But every time a man attempted to kiss me, I became cold as ice. Finally, I stopped going out altogether and became deeply depressed.

Fortunately, my depression did not interfere with my ability to perform at the Two O'Clock Club nor with my ability to make money. Still, I was terribly unhappy. I felt that there was a part of my life that was missing, and for the first time I could find no solution. I began to question who I was, where I was going, what I had done, and spent long hours wondering about what I had accomplished, if anything. In the final analysis, I always concluded, miserably, that I had been a rather selfish person, that almost everything I had done had been for me alone.

One night, I expressed these thoughts to my housekeeper, a kind and considerate woman who was always much concerned about my well-being. She listened intently, and when I finished, she looked at me and said, ''Blaze, you are still a young woman, a very attractive woman, and a very intelligent woman. If you want to do something with your life, why don't you get involved with religious or charitable activities? There are so many things that you could get involved in here in the city of Baltimore to help others if that's what you sincerely want to do.''

The following weekend I asked my sister Debbie, who was living with me and working at the Two O'Clock Club, to drive me back to Twelve Pole Creek to see my mother. My parents had moved a few years earlier from our cabin in Newground Hollow to a two-story white farmhouse beside the main highway. I told my mother when I arrived that I had come home to think. The next morning I got up at daylight, put on a pair of slacks, and told her that I was going to the cabin back in Newground Hollow and would probably be gone all day. She looked at me in amazement but said nothing.

It was the first time that I had been back to the cabin in more than ten years. The path up the mountain had grown over with small bushes, and all the pasture lands and gardens were covered with young poplar timber. It took me more than an hour to reach the cabin. Everything in the house had been moved out except an old broken-down rocking chair, which I carried to the front porch.

I sat there in the rocking chair for almost five hours with my eyes closed, listening to the birds and thinking about myself and my childhood. My grandpa, ol' Twelve-Toed John Fleming, Aunt Sally Slater—my whole early life and all the people in it unraveled before me. I thought about Clarice Meadows, a coal miner's widow who had gone to school with me. Clarice had remained in the hollow and married a local boy. They had nine children when he was mortally wounded in a slate fall. She now lived in a dilapidated shack, surviving on government welfare.

Clarice was not much different from others who had decided to stay along the creek. Most lived in shacks, surviving on food stamps and the welfare checks that the government passed out each month. They had no choice; there were no jobs to be had. Two or three of my classmates had left the hollow and gone to Detroit where they worked in automobile factories. Like me, they would come back home as often as possible to visit with relatives. It was amazing how little life on Twelve Pole Creek changed from one visit to another. It was as if everything were standing still.

In many ways I was lucky, I told myself. I could very easily have been like Clarice or any one of the other girls who had chosen to stay behind. Or I could have been the girl my brother John had told me about the night before, when I got home. Of course, he had thought the story was terribly funny. The woman's husband had lost ninety dollars in a poker game. It was all they had. Then, instead of coming home, he had slipped off to the house of another man's wife and got caught in bed, stark naked. When he did get home, all scarred from battle, his wife hit him over the head with a dough roller. That gash required fourteen stitches. But although it was the fourth time the same thing had happened, they made up the next day.

By midafternoon, I had carefully thought out what I was going to do with the rest of my life, or at least a goodly portion of it, and I had decided to devote a sizable hunk of my time when I wasn't working to helping other people. My housekeeper's suggestion had started it. But it was just sitting on the cabin porch rocking that I realized what I could and was going to do with myself.

Knowing what I had to do made me feel like a different person. I sang and whistled as I ran down the mountain path to the house. When I told my mother, she grabbed me and hugged me.

15

As June and I drove to the Two O'Clock Club, torrents of rain whipped against the car. The windshield wipers were clapping at high speed, but it was still almost impossible to see the road. I had never learned to drive an automobile, so June, who was tending bar for me at the Two O'Clock Club, always stopped by promptly at seven each evening to bring me to the club. She had moved to Baltimore several years before, after finally getting up enough nerve to leave her husband, Luther, who was constantly beating the hell out of her. Once in Baltimore, she had remarried—a thoughtful and devoted man who had been very kind to both June and her children. But shortly after they were married, he had been killed in an automobile accident. It was rough on June, and it took her a long time to get over it. June was a whiz as a bartender. Her personality and her businesslike manner made her exceptionally good with the type of customers who frequent the Two O'Clock Club. She could handle any situation. She never lost her cool.

As June fought the car through the rain and the traffic, she glanced over and said, "For all the good it'll do us, I guess we might as well have stayed home tonight. This rain is going to keep everybody off The Block. You know, it's been raining for about seven or eight days straight now, hasn't it?"

"Yes," I replied. "Must be off Hurricane Agnes. It sure is bad for business. It could be worse, though, you know. Just think if we were down in those Southern states where it really hit. I guess we'd have something to gripe about."

"I guess you're right, Blaze."

To our surprise, the Two O'Clock Club was about half filled that night despite the inclement weather. Ordinarily, I spend most of my time between shows out front socializing with the customers. But for some reason or another, probably just the continuing bad weather, I was in a rather melancholy mood and had been for the entire day. I just sat back in my dressing room. The band was playing "Summertime." The organ music was vibrating through the thin walls, and the drums were flailing away, keeping time with the organ's bump-and-grind beat. Only five of my girls had shown up. I guessed that the heavy rain, or perhaps a late party the night before, had kept the other two away.

As Sharon, the emcee who had been with me since I first purchased the Two O'Clock Club, began to sing an oldie from times past, I reached over, pulled a cigarette from my purse, and leaned back for a smoke. I had about ten minutes before I would go on for my second performance of the evening. The torrents of rain beating against the outside wall of the Two O'Clock Club seemed to be keeping time with the drums.

I waited for the long drum roll that ended with Sharon's introduction: "Ladies and Gentlemen, it's Starr time! You have seen her on television, you have read about her in newspapers, you have looked at her pictures in international magazines, and now you have the opportunity to see her in person! I give you the Queen of Burlesque, Blaze Starr!''

There was the usual applause as I rushed onto the stage, just as I had done thousands of times before, wearing the mink that Governor Earl had bought for me years earlier in New Orleans and puffing a cigarette in a long holder. I danced down to the end of the stage as I threw off my coat and dragged it behind me. There were eight or ten middle-aged men, well-dressed in business suits, sitting to the right of the stage. No doubt they were in Baltimore on business and had chosen the Two O'Clock Club for their night out on the town. To my left sat three or four soldiers. Two young guys with long beards and leather jackets sat at the far end of the stage sipping bottles of beer. They looked like they belonged to a motorcycle gang. Three or four of June's customers at the far end of the room had turned their bar stools around to catch the act.

As I danced back and forth across the stage, I noticed that Carl Remburg had moved up closer to get as good a view as possible of my performance. He was just standing there, squinting at the glare of the stage lights. Carl, probably my greatest admirer, worked as custodian of a federal building in Essex County, New York, and once a month when he had saved his money, he would catch a bus and ride all the way to Baltimore just to visit with me at the Two O'Clock Club. The first time he came in, he had walked up and said, ''Miss Starr, may I have your autograph?'' He was nervous and shaking. Finally, he told me that he had come all the way from New York by bus just to see me. He had been reading about me for years and said that he was fascinated by what he had read about me. He carried a copy of a 1964 *Esquire* Magazine in which I had again been featured and held it up for me to see. At first, I thought he was joking, but it didn't take long to see the sincerity in his eyes and on his face.

For over three years now, Carl had been coming to the Two O'Clock Club once a month, carrying a little overnight case, watching the show, and then, after a few hours of sleep, catching the bus back to New York. After I learned how he made his living cleaning the bathrooms in the federal building, and how little he was paid, I told the girls never to charge him for a drink. He always wanted to pay, but I always refused. I felt that if a man saved his money and came that far just to see me, I certainly wouldn't have the nerve to take his money. The least I could do was to give him a drink when he came in.

When the mink coat hit the floor, I winked at one of the eight distinguished-looking businessmen and said, "That's all right, honey, that guy over there is going to buy me a new mink. Aren't you, honey?" I teased his companion. "And make me work for it. I love my work," I sang out. "I do, I do."

Carl continued to watch every move I made, grinning from ear to ear. Part of my act was allowing one of the male customers to come up and pull a rose from between my breasts with his teeth. This evening, I decided that I would let Carl be the one. I called out my usual line, "It's flower-pickin' time in the hills!" and motioned to him and asked if he would like to pick a flower. He came forward with dazzling speed and stood just below me on the stage stretching down the length of the club as if he could not believe that I had selected him. I bent forward, and Carl grabbed onto the rose with his teeth. I pulled his head forward and held him. I could feel him breathing deeply, and his body trembled. There was laughter and clapping from throughout the room, all coming from different isolated spots where groups had concentrated. I released Carl, and he moved back off the stage, almost stunned. I knew he would tell that story to all his co-workers in New York.

I also knew that he would preserve that rose probably as long as he lived.

With that part of my act completed, I moved into my old, simulated flame routine on the couch, and a few minutes later, I was bouncing off stage again to the applause and approval of the small crowd. Just as I approached my dressing room, I was told by one of the workers that Debbie was on the telephone from the house and that she sounded terribly upset. I hurried to the phone, wondering what was wrong. Perhaps it was John, her ten-year-old son. Maybe he was sick. When I reached the phone, Debbie was hysterical.

"What's wrong? Stop crying and tell me. What's wrong?" I asked.

"The house is flooding, Blaze. The house is flooding. The water is already three feet in the house in some places."

"Oh, my God, that's impossible," I thought, but then I remembered how the small creek behind my place had been rising for days past. Nothing like this had ever happened in that neighborhood, but it wasn't impossible. "Can you get out?" I asked.

"Yes, we are leaving now. There are some men here with a boat, and we are leaving. Don't worry about us. But I thought I'd better call and tell you. It looks like the whole house is going to be wrecked."

"I'll be there as soon as I can get there. Just get John and don't worry about anything else in the house. Just get John and yourself out of there."

She assured me that she and John were all right and would be taken to safety momentarily by the men in the boat.

It took me only ten or fifteen minutes to close the club, apologizing for the inconvenience and explaining that my house in the suburbs of Baltimore was being flooded by the creek that ran behind it. "Please leave quickly," I asked the customers. "I have to get there as soon as possible." But even though we moved as fast as we could, by the time June and I arrived at Queen Anne Road, we could only get the car to within four blocks of my house. Spotlights were beaming, and I could see that the water had already raised up halfway to the front windows.

Everything I had worked for, everything that I owned, was inside my house, and it was being destroyed. All the newspaper clippings, all the pictures that traced my career, all the furniture that I had so carefully selected, all my jewelry that hadn't been stolen, all the other gifts that Earl Long had given me, all would be destroyed, I thought.

As I waded up Queen Anne Road, with water above my knees, I saw that my neighbors' homes, which were located in a row beside the creek, were flooded as badly as mine. I heard a dog whining from inside a neighbor's garage. It sounded terribly frightened. Without thinking, I waded towards the garage door in order to open it and free the dog. Just as I grabbed his chain, the water rose again suddenly, and it dawned on me belatedly that I had no business fooling around in a flood. I couldn't even swim. I tied the dog to my waist, then lay on my back hoping to stay afloat until I could once again get my feet on the ground. The dog was pulling one way, and I was pulling the other. I still don't know whether it was I who saved the dog, or the dog who saved me. But shortly we were once again on ground where I could stand. My gown was soaked, naturally, and some of the bystanders who came to help me to my feet thought I was crazy. But I have always been very fond of dogs, and I just couldn't stand hearing the poor thing bark and suffer, knowing how frightened he was.

One of the neighbors told us that Debbie and John were safe on higher ground. But it was thirty minutes before June and I were reunited with them. Debbie was crying, and so was John. I told them to cheer up, all was not lost.

There was no need to cry. We were safe and together. But I felt awful about what was happening to my house.

Early the next morning, after an entire night without sleep, June and I walked down Queen Anne Road to survey the damage. The water had receded, and there was nothing but thick ugly mud covering the entire lawn. The swimming pool was completely filled with black mud. The iron picket fence around the property had been totally destroyed, wrenched into useless loops by the current. My house itself had been practically split in two, windows were broken out, and some of the furniture had washed out on the lawn. That afternoon, the National Guard moved in, and with the help of friends, we began the enormous task of cleaning up the mess. The only things in the house that were not badly damaged or completely destroyed were my guitar and five-string banjo. I was elated when I saw the banjo lying dry as could be on one of the foam cushions that had floated up off the couch. Evidently as the water rose in the house, the foam cushion just rose with it with my banjo lying snug on top. It was unharmed, as was the guitar, which had been lying on another cushion. I picked up the banjo and strummed a few notes in a pretty forlorn effort to keep up my spirits. Everything else in the house was a sodden mess.

I did all I could that first morning at my house, then jumped in to help some of the neighbors clean up their messes. We continued this from one house to the next for a week or longer, getting the wrecked furniture out. It was days before I was able to move back into my house, and even then there was still dried mud and dust all over the place. I knew it was going to be a long, hard task to restore the house to its former grandeur. But I certainly was not prepared to abandon it.

All during the clean-up, I kept the Two O'Clock Club open every night, although I soon became exhausted working at the club every night and working all day every day in the ruined house. Business all along The Block for one reason or another was falling off rapidly, and some nights I was performing to an almost empty house. I fought desperately to maintain my morale, but as the weeks went by I became as concerned with the financial plight of the Two O'Clock Club as with the condition of the house. More than ever, I needed money to restore the house, and day by day my problems in both places seemed to mount rather than dissipate.

The Block had been in increasing financial trouble since the mid-1960s, but now it appeared to be suddenly much worse. Criminal elements had moved in. New club owners and new entrepreneurs began to appear, people whom I had never seen before, and dirty-book stores and peep-show places began to open. Dope addicts roamed the street, and female impersonators moved more and more openly from club to club seeking out the unsuspecting males. Fights erupted among the amusement supply companies, each trying to get its twenty-five-cent peep shows into the various clubs and bookstores that lined both sides of the street. In some instances rival companies threw dirty-movie machines in the gutter and broke them up with sledge hammers. Word spread throughout Baltimore that it was unsafe to take your girlfriend or wife to visit even one of the few remaining respectable places, such as the Two O'Clock Club.

A new federal task force moved in on The Block in an effort to seek out any organized crime that might have penetrated the legitimate burlesque clubs. There was absolute fear among the club owners that they would soon be closed down. In fact, practically every club owner experienced a wave of paranoia when the federal task force was even mentioned. I felt it, too, despite the fact that I had always maintained a respectable club, one that a husband would feel perfectly free to bring his wife to. June's two daughters, who lately had joined us, were nice girls.

Nobody I hired from outside the family was allowed to hustle the customers, and June saw to it that the drinks were never watered. Unlike many of the other club owners on The Block, I would never allow my girls to take off all their clothes. But we were in trouble, anyway, and I knew it.

On top of everything else, there was still another reason why business was continuing to decline. The city had announced plans for urban renewal that included razing The Block. There had been a great deal of publicity concerning this program in the papers. Many people got the mistaken idea the The Block, and the Two O'Clock Club along with it, had been renewed into oblivion.

Nothing seemed to be going right. My house still smelled of the flood. No amount of scrubbing with the strongest disinfectants seemed to get rid of the lingering nasty odor of mud. My club that I had bought so confidently, sure that Mr. Goodman's fears for the future of The Block were unfounded, was in trouble. Despite my hardest efforts to keep it lively and full of customers without relaxing the standards I had set for it, I was beginning to lose money on its operation. Only my charitable work, which I had set myself to do and had stuck to regularly ever since the day three years before when I had come down out of Newground Hollow knowing what I had to do, was giving me any satisfaction. And now I was beginning to wonder how soon charity might have to begin all over again at home.

16

It was around this time that I received a call from Reverend Bob Harrington, the Bourbon Street preacher who had gained national fame by doing most of his preaching in the bars and clubs of Bourbon Street in New Orleans. I guess I had been too busy to hear about him, what with one thing and another. So I was absolutely surprised when he called the Two O'Clock Club and asked for me one evening. I was even more surprised when he said that he would like to come to the club and preach.

"Preacher," I said, "I don't want to be rude, but I think you have flipped. Who ever heard tell of a preacher coming to a burlesque club to preach? Why, they would run me off The Block if I allowed you to come in here."

He attempted to explain to me that he had been successful in other areas, that he believed in taking his message to the sinners and felt the sinners were located in just such places as Baltimore's famous Block.

After a few minutes' discussion with him on the phone, I finally realized that the man was sincere in his request.

However, I told him that I had too much trouble with all the female impersonators and perverts who were going around harassing some of my customers even to think about what would happen if I brought in a preacher. It was beyond my imagination. I turned him down.

But the very next day his publicity manager, Brother Bill as he identified himself, called and once again requested that Brother Bob be allowed to come and preach at the Two O'Clock Club. Word had already gotten out among the other club owners that I was getting ready to bring in a preacher, and I had received a call earlier in the day warning me that I could consider myself in trouble if I did. The caller had said that The Block had enough trouble with the federal people probing into everybody's affairs, and if I brought in a preacher, it would just be the end of everything.

Needless to say, that telephone conversation ran through my mind as Brother Bill was making his persuasive argument that I should allow Brother Bob to come in and preach that evening. In truth, I had almost made up my mind after that call to get in touch with Brother Bob myself and invite him in. The one thing I dislike more than anything else is having someone call me anonymously and threaten me.

Brother Bill was obviously surprised when I told him that I would agree to allow Brother Bob to come in and preach, but for no longer than fifteen minutes. "Terrific!" he said. "That is terrific! The Lord will bless you. We will be there at eleven."

As I hung up the phone, I immediately asked myself, "What in the hell have you done now, Blaze? How could you allow your desire to get even with the anonymous caller to get the best of you?" For a moment I thought about phoning Brother Bill back and calling the whole thing off. But I decided that having made the decision I would stick with it, regardless of what happened.

That evening I dressed as usual in a low-cut gown and was getting ready for my first performance when the federal task force appeared in the Two O'Clock Club. The leader of the group came up to me and said that he would prefer that I close the club down for some hours to allow them to investigate to see whether I was involved in any illicit activity. He attempted to be apologetic and said it was part of his duty and his assignment to investigate each of the clubs and he was sorry to cause any inconvenience.

I promptly went to the stage microphone and announced what was happening. What customers I had left hurriedly, and we locked the doors. I pretended not to be nervous, but you never know when someone has slipped in a bottle of whiskey that is half watered or some other illicit gimmick that might be hidden on the premises. They searched throughout the entire club while I sat agonizing in my dressing room awaiting their verdict. An hour and a half passed, and they were still busily searching. All this time, though I was unaware of it, Brother Bob Harrington and his entire crew were waiting outside to get into the club. With them were reporters from the *Baltimore Sun* and also some television people from the local stations who had been covering Reverend Bob's appearance in Baltimore. He had been preaching all week at the civic center. Someone had told them all that the federal task force was inside and that the club had been closed temporarily.

Finally, after what seemed to be an eternity, the leader of the task force came up and apologized again and left without telling me anything whatsoever. As I opened the door for the federal men to leave, Reverend Bob and his group poured in. As he was introduced to me by Brother Bill, I apologized for the inconvenience that we had caused.

Brother Bob was quite a man, I thought, with his gray, wavy hair accenting his terribly handsome face. He wore a white suit and carried a Bible. I was terribly nervous, to say the least. I suddenly thought about Grandma Fannie and her religion, and I figured she'd roll over in her grave if she knew that I had allowed one of those slick evangelist preachers she had always despised so much to come in and preach at the Two O'Clock Club. I knew there was no way on earth that I could ever have convinced her that this man was sincere. I could just imagine what she would say about him, that he was out for the money, not for the Lord. I didn't know what his game was. But I figured I was going to find out sooner or later. He took my hand and said that the Lord would bless me for allowing him to come in and bring his services to the people.

The Two O'Clock Club began to fill back up in a short time. In fact, there was an unusually large crowd, probably because of the presence of the television cameras. Elaine, a young black-haired stripper, had already gone into her act and was clad only in her G-string and pasties as she wiggled from one end of the stage to the other. Some of the young strippers don't use the bump-and-grind method we older strippers learned and pursued. Their technique is more or less a combination of modern dance and the old bump-and-grind. Its quite effective, and the audience usually approves.

I didn't know exactly how Brother Bob was going to react to the almost naked girl on stage. It didn't seem likely he would approve of her technique. But it didn't seem to bother him. He waited patiently until the young dancer completed her performance, and then I went with him on stage and introduced him. I explained to the audience that I thought it was a hell of a place for a preacher to be, but this one had been persistent, and I thought just out of curiosity I would bring him in. "Now he wants to speak to everyone," I said, "so if you'll just be patient, we'll let him say his piece."

Brother Bob's preaching was a little different from what I had anticipated. He was not a hellfire-and-damnation preacher like I had been accustomed to back in the mountains of West Virginia. Rather, he talked to the customers about the various problems that mankind in general was facing. Of course, it wound up with the same theme, that the only way that we could solve our problems was with the help of God, by giving our souls to God. He was a magnetic speaker, and the more I listened to him, the more intent I became. The television cameras were grinding away as he spoke, cameras flashed, and the newspaper reporters went around taking notes and observing the crowd.

Altogether, he spoke for about fifteen minutes, and at the end to my amazement practically everyone stood up and applauded the man. Before he left that evening, he made me promise that I would appear with him at the civic center on Sunday. I accepted the invitation without much thought.

The papers the next day carried pictures of Brother Bob and me standing at the Two O'Clock Club. He had a big smile on his face, and the Bible was very visible. The papers also carried the story that Blaze Starr, the Queen of Burlesque, would be at the civic center with the Reverend Bob Harrington. It gave the impression that I was about to be saved by the Reverend. I was far from being saved, but I was certainly impressed.

There were thousands of people at the civic center when I walked down the aisle amidst a standing ovation to the front where Reverend Bob had set up his pulpit. I still can't decide what the audience might have been imagining, but never before in my life had I experienced the kind of applause and the handshaking that I did that day. It gave me a very strange feeling, one of the strangest I had ever felt, entirely different from that of performing as a stripper. As I walked forward, Reverend Bob left the pulpit, met me at the end of the aisle, and shook my hand. ''God bless you," he said. "God bless you." I turned to the crowd and waved.

Brother Bob did some mighty preaching that day. He told about how he had cleaned up some of the strip clubs down in New Orleans and said that one of his ambitions was to close all the strip joints all over the United States, to rid the nation of its dens of iniquity. He didn't say it in exactly those words, but that was his meaning. He mentioned my name a time or two, and I sat there a little tense as he spoke.

As he finished, the choir began singing an old-time hymn, and Brother Bob made his plea to the sinners as the money trays were passed around. It seemed that everyone's eyes were fastened on me, and I assume they expected me to go forth and give my soul to God, or at least to Brother Bob.

I wasn't about to go that far. I must admit that he was one of the most persuasive men I have ever met, but as far as I was concerned, I couldn't run a strip club and be a child of God. Besides, I had gotten over my problem with men and was now happily dating a very good-looking man with whom I was very much impressed. I figured I had a lot of "sinning" to do before I was ready to settle down, things that I wasn't going to be allowed to do if I "gave my heart to God" according to Brother Bob.

After the service, Brother Bob continued trying to get me to join his crusade, to "get right with God," and to do what he described as "good things" for humanity. Brother Bill talked about my joining his staff as a publicity agent for the crusade. I said, "Man, I can't do that. I just can't give myself to this kind of work without first giving my soul to God. I'm just not ready to do it." Brother Bob said he would keep trying, that one day he was going to save me, and I would make a dandy for the Lord when he did.

I called my mother that night and told her what had

happened and all about my experience at the Baltimore civic center. I told her what a strong and strange feeling I had had when I walked down the aisle. I discussed the entire matter with her and told her that Brother Bob had offered me a very good salary if I would join his crusade and become a publicity agent working with Brother Bill, going into the towns before Reverend Bob appeared, and helping to set up the revivals and promote them. It was more money than I was making as a stripper.

My mother was terribly upset. She said that while she didn't know anything about Reverend Bob and all his motives, she did know I surely ought to be careful about accepting any such offer to do God's work for a salary. Grandma Fannie had never accepted one penny for all her religious work, she said, and she herself was more than a little concerned about people who made their living in that manner.

I told her I didn't think I was really serious about joining Reverend Harrington's campaign, but that I had at least thought I ought to discuss it with her, and that I personally felt that Reverend Bob was a good man trying to do good deeds. She told me I was old enough to make up my own mind.

I stayed at the Two O'Clock Club.

17

Business went from bad to worse all through that summer. I kept getting more and more nervous and tired and just generally feeling downright snakebit. Finally, after losing money night after night, I decided that I was going to lock up the club, at least for a while, and try just staying home to get my house back in order. There was no need losing what money I had earned and what money I had saved. I thought perhaps later I could find myself a new business outside The Block area—maybe a fried chicken place where I could have country music with a little burlesque thrown in. Maybe I could move into a shopping center and begin something new.

For the next six months, I worked feverishly in an effort to rebuild my house. It was slow, but soon it began to take on its former shape. I got my old childhood sweetheart, Jethro Spaulding, who had recently divorced his wife, to come up from Twelve Pole Creek and help me with some of the carpentry work. And when we weren't working on the house, Jethro and I were ''picking and singing'' on the guitar and banjo. I even wrote three or four songs during the time, which probably reflected the mood I was in. One, which I call "38 Double D," went like this:

> In the hills of West Virginia
> There's a place called Wilsondale
> Long ago I lived there
> And my name was Fannie Belle
> I hoed corn in the cornfields
> Oh, Lord, what a pity
> I dug ginseng in the mountains
> For a ticket to the city.
> I said goodbye Mamma
> You're gonna be proud of me
> You said if I kept on growin'
> I'd be a 38 double D
> Well, I'm a 38 double D
> And they all come to look at me
> And if inches really count
> Then I'm in luck from A to Z.
>
> So hello Mamma
> I went out and done my thing
> I've got a bunch of mink coats
> And a dozen diamond rings.
> But every night when I come home
> I feel so all alone
> Wish I was diggin' ginseng
> In the mountains way back home.
>
> I miss those all-day meetin's
> With dinner on the ground
> I miss my country music
> With the kin folks comin' round
> So look for me Mamma

I'll be comin' soon
I'll be drinkin' my corn liquor
And a howlin' at the moon.

Yes, I'm a 38 double D
They all come to look at me
And if inches really count
Then I'm in luck from A to Z.

The day Jethro was putting the final touches on the last coat of paint in the living room, I spent a lot of time talking on the phone. When I came in from the bedroom, he looked down at me from the stepladder and said, "Reckon if you had stayed on that phone much longer, I would have finished the whole room."

"You're not going to believe it when I tell you," I said.

"What do you mean I ain't going to believe it? You stay on that phone half the time. What makes this time so different?" He dipped the roller into the paint tray.

"As a matter of fact, I don't believe it, either."

"Aw, damn it, Fannie Belle, what makes you go on like that? Why don't you come on out with it? Is your mother coming up or something?"

"Oh, no. It's not anything like that. What would you think if I told you I am going to reopen the Two O'Clock Club?"

Jethro started to climb down from the ladder. "No kidding?"

"No kidding. But I didn't tell you to stop painting."

"Never you mind, Fannie Belle, I'll finish the painting. But right now I'm going to fix us a big drink of liquor. It ain't every day a person like you gets her sense back all of a sudden. Anyways, I was looking for some kind of excuse to have another drink."

He went into the kitchen and yelled out, "You got anything to chase this liquor with, Fannie?"

"Yeah, there's some Coke in the bottom of the refrigerator."

Jethro came back into the room carrying a fifth of Jack Daniel's and a Coke. He was planning to catch the bus back to West Virginia the next week. He said he had a job in a coal mine. He broke the seal on the whiskey and turned the bottle to his lips, took a long gulp, and followed it with a swig of Coke. As he wiped his mouth on his shirt sleeve, he looked at me and said, "Do you have any idea when you're going to open up again?"

"As soon as I can get the place redecorated. It's got to look near as good as this does so I won't be tempted to go on staying home all the time. I got some calls from some businessmen last week who are encouraging me to reopen. That was one of them I was just talking to again. They say The Block's really calmed down during the last few months. The police have gone in and arrested a lot of the drug pushers, and they say the women impersonators have been scattered to kingdom come. One of them told me that The Block was just not the same without the Two O'Clock Club. Besides, all the funds for urban renewal have been frozen now, so it'll be at least five years before the subject of razing it will come up again. I've really been thinking about it a lot lately, and it's just not time yet to hang up my G-string for keeps. Besides, there's Debbie and June, and June's two daughters to think of. There's a second generation of Fleming girls stripping now. Even June's littlest, who's just seven, vows she's going to be a stripper like her Aunt Blaze. You might say we Fleming girls have a tradition to keep up."

"You've got a good point there, Fannie Belle. You may just have a good point there."

"Yeah, I've been thinking about it pretty strongly. I tell you, I've been getting awfully tired of being all holed up here like some kind of hibernating bear. And I'm getting fat just lying around and painting. This winter has really been rough on me. I know there's a lot of things I ought to do, like going through all these waterlogged clippings and photograph albums to see what I can salvage. But it just upsets me so much I can't. I thought about starting a new business, but Debbie and I went all over the Baltimore suburbs trying to find a building in one of the shopping centers where we could rent space to put in a fried chicken place. But every time a real estate man found out who I was, he jacked up the price until we couldn't afford it. I guess they were afraid we would corrupt their shopping centers. Or maybe they just thought I was loaded with money. But anyway, it never really worked out.''

Jethro gulped down another shot of Jack Daniel's and once again chased it with the Coke. Looking over at me, he asked, ''Have you called your mother and told her?''

''Well, of course not, Jethro. I've been standing here talking to you ever since I got the call.''

''Why don't you run and do it?'' he suggested.

I went into the bedroom and called my mother to tell her the news. As I had expected, she was pleased to hear I was going back to work, and we talked a long time about all the new ideas I suddenly seemed to have for fixing up the club.

I came back into the living room to find Jethro all sprawled out on the couch. He had already drunk about half the bottle of Jack Daniel's and was still clutching the remainder. I walked over and said, ''You'd best give me that, young man, before you get so drunk you can't walk.''

''Aw, Fannie Belle, that Jack Daniel's ain't going to faze me. Now if I had some of that West Virginia moonshine, you might have something to worry about.''

"Well, anyway, I'm going to take it and put it in the kitchen. You've still got some painting to do so you might as well get yourself back up on that ladder and get to it."

"Oh, curses! Can't we even take time out to celebrate?"

"We've got plenty of time to celebrate. Right now, though, we'd better finish getting this house painted 'cause I've got a lot of other things to do."

Jethro crawled back up on the ladder, mumbling a little because I had taken his bottle from him. I grabbed my brush and began to trim around the baseboards and door facings as we continued to chat back and forth.

"You remember that time that you whipped Sam Workman in the tea patch over me?" I asked.

"Sure do. Those were the good old days, Fannie."

"Yeah, those were the good old days. It's fun to just think back what a great time we had, Jethro. Say, is Aunt Sally Slater still living?" I asked.

"I reckon so. The last time I was up in Williamson, I ran into one of her nephews, and he said she was still doing pretty good. Been a little sickly previous, but other than that just fine."

"I think Aunt Sally is one of the finest women that I have ever known."

"Yeah, she sure is a fine woman. But I'll tell you one thing. She sure in the hell could swing a mean hickory switch when she got mad. I thought she was near going to kill me that time I whipped Sam."

"Well, you deserved it, didn't you?" I laughed.

"Maybe so, but not near as hard as she hit me."

"What are you going to do with yourself, Jethro, when you go back to West Virginia?"

"Well, since me and the old woman got divorced, I've kinda got my eye set on another girl back there in the hollow. And I reckon I'll just go back to that job in the mines and settle down and marry her."

"Who is she, Jethro?"

"Oh, I don't think you'd know her if I told you."

"Reckon she'll be able to handle you?"

"There ain't no goddamn woman going to handle Jethro Spaulding! I'll tell you that right now, Fannie Belle. You ought to know me well enough by now to know that there ain't no damn woman going to handle this man!"

"What do you mean, Jethro? Hasn't women's lib found Twelve Pole Creek yet?"

"Women's lib, hell! That's the biggest bunch of crap I ever heard of. These goddamn women are all trying to act like they're a bunch of men or something. Jesus Christ! Don't you know that a man is born superior to a woman? I've been hearing about all this stuff on television, but I'll tell you one damn thing, a woman's place is in the home. It's just like it says there in the Bible. Any fool knows a man is superior to a woman. If he wasn't, the Lord would have took a rib out of Eve to make Adam." Jethro quit painting and leaned back against the ladder, looking mad, and I couldn't help but laugh.

"What the hell are you laughing about? You ain't one of them women liberators, are you?"

"Jethro, I've been practicing women's lib ever since I was near about fourteen years old and picked up that piece of stove wood and hit June's husband, Luther, over the head to keep him from beating the hell out of her. I sure fixed him up. I left him lying there on the floor. He was out for about ten minutes, and when he came to, he sat over in the corner like a little boy and didn't say another word to June. I'll tell you, Jethro, I've learned one hell of a lot about men in my lifetime. They're all right to take to bed, but you sure better never let them get a stranglehold on you. I've never let myself be dictated to by any male chauvinist.''

"Now, Fannie Belle, you ain't going to peddle that kind of fool stuff on me. Maybe that's the way it is up here in the city, but down home when we tell one of our women to do something, they'd better do it. Why, my God, if you gave women everything they want, they'd be trying to take our jobs in the coal mines before it was over with.''

"So why shouldn't they work in the coal mines if that's what they want to do?''

"Well, God a'mighty! Now, how in the hell do you think a woman is going to be able to go back there in the mines and mine coal like a man, back under that mountain two miles, standing in thirty-six inches of coal?''

"But she's the one who should be able to decide whether she can do it, not you.''

"Well, I know damn well she can't do it.''

"You've never really given her a chance to do it. You don't know. Jethro, I do believe you're just impossible.''

"Impossible, hell! Look at you, Fannie Belle. If there's ever been a woman that took advantage of men, it's you. Where do you think you'd have been if you hadn't had them big tits to show around and make a living with?''

"Well, okay, I grant you, but what you don't understand, Jethro, is that all my life I've done what I want to do, and I haven't been afraid to admit to myself or anybody that I love stripping. If I'm taking advantage, I'm just using what God gave me. It could have been some other kind of gift, and then it would have been up to me to use that. But I got big boobs, and I'm thankful. They give me the kind of chance every women would like to have.''

"What do you mean?''

"Well, you see, Jethro, a lot of women don't do what they want to do because they feel that society would frown on them. It could be a lot of different things they could do. Even now, there's a lot of young girls that really would like to get married and settle down, but they're scared to because all this emphasis on being liberated is a new kind of threat on them."

"You're losin' me, Fannie Belle."

"Yeah, well I haven't thought it all out. But I'll tell you something else, Jethro. Every woman would love to be a stripper. They'd all love to get up on the stage in the Two O'Clock Club and prance back and forth taking their clothes off while the men whistled and yelled at them."

"You mean to tell me you think every woman would like to get up like you Fleming girls and pull her clothes off in public?"

"Yes, I'm telling you just that. Sure my big set of tits have got me where I am. But the point is I would have been a fool not to have taken advantage of a well-endowed body just because a lot of people frowned on the idea."

"So you take advantage of us men. We get in the clubs and get all worked up watching you women strip."

"Okay, but men need a person like me. They need strippers, and they need places like the Two O'Clock Club where they can go to fantasize. They can come in and watch me and the other strippers take our clothes off and get all worked up, like you said, and they can go home then and make made passionate love to their wives. Of course, their wives ought to wise up. A woman ought to wear a negligée and dress up for her man—be his own personal stripper. Unfortunately, most of them look their worst around their old man and wait until they're going out somewhere that another guy can look at them before they get dolled up and look their Sunday best."

"Well, I guess I have to agree with you on that last

point," Jethro said, smiling. "Goddamn, Fannie Belle, you talk so much you ought to put all your ideas in a book and just hand it out to people." He grinned. "But I still think a woman's rightful place is in the house."

"Well, that's your belief. Me, I'm getting out of mine. And I may just write a book about my life. Don't you be surprised if I do just that, Jethro Spaulding. There's a fellow from down home who's been wanting me to. I may just do it."

The following Friday, June and I drove Jethro to the bus station, and on our way back we stopped by the Two O'Clock Club and began putting into effect our plans to redecorate it for the second time in three years. June was almost as excited over the prospect of reopening as I was.

By early May, the club was ready to go, and there was a large crowd on opening night. Many of the old regulars dropped by to wish me well, and everyone on The Block sent flowers. Even Polack Johnny who has a hotdog stand near the Two O'Clock Club, sent me two dozen long-stemmed red roses. I always stop by to have a hotdog with him every night. I love hotdogs.

There was an air of excitement that had not existed on The Block for some time. My morale had never been higher. And about thirty minutes before I was ready to perform my second act of the evening, I received an unexpected and unannounced visit from Brother Bob. By an astonishing coincidence the opening of the club and his revival in Baltimore happened at the same time. One of the girls came running back to the dressing room, yelling, "Blaze! Brother Bob is here!"

"You're kidding."

"Yeah, he's here, television people and everybody."

"Well, I'll be damned!"

I rushed out to the front of the club, and sure enough, there was Brother Bob, standing all decked out in a white suit, his wavy hair flocking down, hiding his ears. He was already passing out pamphlets to all the customers who were sitting at June's bar.

I rushed up to greet him. The television cameras were grinding, and the flashbulbs were lighting up the whole club. I was happy to see him, and we shook hands as he said, "Every time I come to see you, I'm getting you a little closer to the Lord."

"This is where I want to be," I said, "right next to the preacher."

Clutching his Bible close to his side and gesturing with his arm, he spoke loudly enough for the television microphone to pick up the conversation. "This one's going to be a dandy for the Lord when we get her converted. She came near one time about two years ago. I haven't lost hope. I don't give up easy, especially when I've got a good fish I want to hook."

"We'll be together one way or another, Brother Bob," I said, as I released his arm so he could continue passing out pamphlets to all the customers.

"In the kingdom of God," he replied. A few minutes later he left amidst a flurry of flashbulbs.

I signed a few autograph pictures for the customers as I made my way back to the dressing room, thinking to myself, "This is kingdom enough for me for the present. It may be pretty raunchy, but it's all mine, and I like the audience." I hurriedly put on my gown and tossed Earl's mink coat over it, then walked to the stage entrance. There was the familiar drum roll as Sharon introduced me:

"Ladies and gentlemen, it's Starr time! You've read about her in international magazines, seen her on television, and tonight we are announcing a new thrill. Soon you will be able to read her life story in her own book. The world's most famous stripper! Here she is in person, the Queen of Burlesque, the one and only, Blaze Starr!"

I just stood there a little extra time listening to the applause. Of all the good things there are in the world, I guess I like best the sound of clapping. Then I picked up the beat of the music, held out my arms in my long red gloves with a single red rose in my hands, and started dancing down the stage between the tables.

AFTERWORD
by Lora Fleming

To me, Blaze Starr is "Sissie." I have never called my second eldest of my children by any other name.

Though she didn't have the things that children think are necessary today, she had a happy childhood among the hills of West Virginia. She walked across a mountain to a little one-room school on Turkey Creek where I had attended school and had taught before my marriage.

If Sissie had been a boy, she probably would have been a great inventor because she was always trying to make or build something. For her to get an idea meant action, even if we had to let the farmwork go a day to help. There was the time she decided to make her younger brother Ray a wagon. She built a wooden box and intended to saw wheels from an oak log to put on it. For this task, she, her older sister June, and I used a cross-cut saw. The rounds we sawed always ended up with a wide side and a narrow side, but being the determined child she was, Sissie wouldn't give up. She selected the four best rounds and drilled a hole through them with a brace and bit. My, how hard she worked. And believe it or not, she made a pretty good wagon.

There was no going to the store in those days and buying fancy food, clothes, or toys like children have now. First, there were the Depression years with no money to buy with. Then there were the World War II years when we had a little money but nothing to buy. We beat the scarcity of food both times by living strictly off our farm. We always had hogs to kill, cows to milk, plenty of chickens, and usually we could sell a few dozen eggs weekly to the local store. With the egg money, we could get coffee and salt and so on. We always grew all of our own fruit and vegetables, using them fresh in the summer and canning everything extra for use during the winter. Sugar was scarce, but Sissie and June made their own candy from molasses or honey. Homemade popcorn balls were often taken to school to help out with the lunch.

Sissie loved to sing and write songs and poetry. One day, she decided to order the harmonica that had been advertised on the radio. Finally, after a month-long wait, the harmonica came in the mail. In only a day or two Sissie was playing any song she wished. She indeed had an ear for music. About a month later, her Uncle Garfield gave her a banjo. She dearly loved this old banjo and tried desperately to pick and sing like her cousin Molly O'Day, who was at that time doing "Single Girl," "Mule-Skinner Blues," "John Henry," and so on over the radio. After many hours of practice, Sissie could really play that banjo, which by now had been played so much that a hole had worn in its skin cover. One of the neighbors told her that if she would get a groundhog skin that he would make a cover for her. So taking her .22 she went to what we all called the groundhog den. This was a large hole under a rock where several groundhogs had been shot when they came out in the afternoon for food. Concealing herself in a clump of bushes, Sissie took up her lonely vigil beside the rock. As the hours passed by, she grew cramped and stiff. She longed to stand a while but didn't dare as she knew one movement would scare the animals and all of her waiting would have been in vain. She dozed a bit finally, and when she opened her eyes, there were three groundhogs at the entrance to the hole, a mama and her two babies. They were behaving just like kids, boxing and playing in the afternoon sun. Quietly, Sissie picked up her gun and walked back down the mountain, shuddering at the thought of what she had almost done. Being a firm believer in God, she says to this day that God was watching over those animals, showing her how happy they all were together.

Not long after that foxes began killing all our chickens, which we had let have the run of the place as all of our gardens were fenced. One day Goodlow, my husband, and Sissie saw a large, red fox run into a hole under a nearby rock. They decided they would smoke it out and then shoot it, putting an end to at least part of the chicken-killing. Goodlow set some feed sacks on fire and put them in the hole. In a few minutes, Sissie's eyes were watering, and she almost strangled on the smoke. She began crying and begging her daddy to stop, saying that it must be awful to be smoked like that. So he took out the sacks, and the foxes continued to kill the chickens.

Like to any normal child, there came a time in Sissie's life when she decided she just had to have a bicycle. Her father and I tried to explain to her that there wasn't enough flat land in the head of Newground Hollow to make buying a bicycle worthwhile. But nothing dimmed her enthusiasm, and she immediately started earning the money with which to buy it. Her Grandma Fannie had taught her to crochet, so she made some pretty doilies that she sold to some of the neighbors. She dug ginseng and sold it to our storekeepers, Eva Maynard and Myrtle Perry. Usually they just gave their customers groceries from the store for the worth of their ginseng. But being the kind ladies they were, and knowing of her desire to buy a bike, they gave her the money so that she could add it to her growing fund. After doing a few washings on a washboard for some of the neighbors, she at last had the money to buy a secondhand bike from Add Spaulding who lived on Turkey Creek. He helped her roll it home up the winding path across the mountain. She didn't keep it long when she realized for herself that it was impossible to ride it in those mountains. So later she sold it to Hattie Adkins, making a neat profit of four dollars.

The woman who now has such a vast wardrobe began school one year with only two dresses. One I ordered from Sears and Roebuck for forty-nine cents and the other I made from bleached dairy feed sacks, appliquéing flowers on the front for trim. Her sister June had the same kind of clothes. Of course, this was during the Depression years, so I guess they were lucky to have that much. Goodlow had been cut off from his job on the Norfolk and Western Railroad, and our only income was what he earned working for the neighbors or on the WPA, a government project. I remember how sad the children were when he finally did get called back to work for the N & W in Portsmouth, Ohio, because this meant his being away from his family for months at a time.

Sissie always loved to write songs and poems. She and her sister June wrote several during their childhood. One that I will always remember was written during the days of World War II, after Japan attacked the United States and so many young men were being drafted. Goodlow had filled out his questionnaire, and we were expecting him to get his call to the army any day. All a body could hear on the radio or read in the newspaper was war and more war. To the little girls, going to war meant certain death. At that time so many in that area were being brought back killed or wounded. With June's help Sissie one day wrote this song, weaving into it parts of a handed-down mountain lullaby that I used to sing to them:

The year was nineteen-forty-one
We were happy day and night,
Then Uncle Sam wrote my daddy
That he must go out and fight.
And each day we girls would pray
That Daddy would return someday
Then we would sing:

Bye-o-baby buntin'
Daddy's gone a hunting'
Going to get a possum skin
To wrap his little babies in.

That's the song my daddy sang to me,
Long ago when he bounced us on his knee.

Then a letter edged in black
Came to our mountain shack
And Mamma cried all night long,
She said, "Sissie, you and June
Better practice another tune
Daddy's going to help the angels sing their song."
Then we would sing:

Bye-o-baby buntin'
Daddy's gone a huntin'
Going to get a possum skin
To wrap his little babies in.

That's the song my daddy sang to me,
Long ago when he bounced us on his knee.

May I add that her father didn't have to go to the army as he was working then as a brakeman for the railroad, and his job qualified as one of vital importance.

As you can see, Sissie was inclined to write, sing, and play since her early childhood. This accounts for her songs and music (of a different tune), which she keeps writing all the time and enjoys so much today.

One by one Sissie and the rest of the children left home, but a big family usually seems to be a close family, and they always came back often to get together with their brothers and sisters. I remember the first time when Sissie came home after she started working in Baltimore. She had not seen the new house Goodlow and I had saved up to purchase, and there was lots of excitement as the younger children and I worked to get everything in order. It was just getting dark, and I didn't hear the bus stop in front of the house. All of a sudden came the barking and whining of the three old dogs Sissie had done her hunting with in the head of the hollow. Running out on the porch I saw Sissie perched in an apple tree while the dogs were rolling and fighting. I started to laugh, but stopped when I saw she was crying her heart out while yelling something about her coat. The dogs finally stopped fighting, and I saw the tattered garment lying on the ground.

Sissie came down out of the tree, dried her eyes, and began to explain the situation to me. She had come across the bridge with a new mink coat draped across her arm. The dogs, thinking it was some wild animal, had started running towards her. Realizing what was happening, she had tried to climb the nearest apple tree to save her coat, but the dogs were too fast for her. The coat was beyond repair, but Sissie's broken heart wasn't. She just began saving her money and later bought another mink coat more beautiful and more expensive than the first.

Sissie dearly loved her father and came to visit him often during his three years of illness prior to his death. She now makes several trips a year to place flowers on his grave and visit with me.

I just wonder what will be the fate of my Sissie, the Blaze Starr of today. Will she turn to writing country songs that will go on through the years? She's talking a lot about that. Will she keep on running the Two O'Clock Club or settle down with a husband? I see some signs that she's looking to find peace with the Lord like her grandma, my mother, that Goodlow and I named her after. No matter what her fate, I do know one thing for certain. She had to have talent to get where she is today. And I'm sure that since this has put her in a position to help others, her life will continue to be rewarding and fulfilling. All because deep down she's still Sissie of Newground Hollow.

Wilsondale, West Virginia
February 1974